Who is

CHARLES

LEVINE?

Who is

CHARLES LEVINE?

A novel
by Jeffrey Saporta

Based on a True Story

This novel is based on a real story, but it is a work of fiction. Charles Levine was a real person, as were Mabel Boll, Clarence Chamberlin, and Giuseppe Bellanca. Dates, events, conversations, and character traits have been changed and enhanced for dramatic purposes. Other than the use of historical figures, any resemblance to actual persons, living or dead, is entirely coincidental.

Dedication

Dedicated to the memory of the Six Million Jews killed in the Holocaust. May The World never forget.

PART I: THE BUSINESSMAN

CHAPTER 1

December 1991

Alaine Pollack lives with her parents, Edith and Philip, in Bethesda, Maryland, a suburb just a few miles outside of Washington D.C. On a cold blustery day, she jumps off her school bus excited to tell her mother what she was taught this day. A precocious and exceedingly intelligent eleven-year-old, she is always proud to relate newfound knowledge.

Her mother opens the back door of their home to let Alaine in. "So, darling what did you learn today?"

"Mom, it was so interesting," she responds breathlessly. "My teacher told our class all about a true American hero—Charles Lindbergh."

1

A wry smile crosses Edith's face. "A hero you say—Charles Lindbergh?"

"Yes, Mom, he was the first person to cross the Atlantic Ocean solo from New York to Paris non-stop in an airplane. It was quite an amazing accomplishment back then."

"I am fully aware of how Charles Lindbergh first became famous, but there is another side of his story that you should know about."

"Oh, what would that be?" Alaine asks, as curious as ever.

"I'm not the one who should tell that story. Go upstairs and ask your Grandfather. I'm sure he will entertain you with quite a tale."

"Grandpa? He's so old and grumpy. What does he know about history?"

"My dear child—he has lived it.".

Charles A. Levine is an old man of 94 years of age. He was born on March 17, 1897. His hard life has made his appearance all the worse. In his youth he was a handsome, robust man, now he is reduced to being an invalid, bent over and unable to walk without the use of a cane. His arms and legs shake uncontrollably, and he speaks in a hoarse whisper. His clothes hang, appearing to be two sizes too large, from his rail-thin body. And Alaine is right, he is grumpy. His wits and memory, though, are as good as a person half his age. Up until two weeks prior, he was living in a homeless shelter, without a penny to his name, just waiting to die.

His daughter, Edith, has not seen him in over 20 years, but after a social worker locates him, Edith, saddened by his appearance and health, insists that he come to live in her house with her husband, Philip, and their daughter. He gladly does so.

Alaine knocks on the door of the attic which Edith has fashioned into a small bedroom. There is no answer. Alaine knocks harder. "I heard you the first time. Go away, I just want to sleep," he answers bitterly.

Alaine is fearful but determined. From behind the closed door, she says "Mom says you can answer some of my questions."

"I said go away, little girl. Who do you think I am— *the answer man*?" he says referring to an expression long since out of use.

"Mom says you know something about Charles Lindbergh."

With the mention of that name, a fierce scowl appears on his face. *If looks could kill,* Lindbergh would be dead all over again. "Did you say Charles Lindbergh?"

"Yes, Grandpa, I learned about him in school today."

The expression on Charles' face now changes to a knowing smirk. He never waivers in his desire to set the record straight about *this great man.* His voice softens, "Come in sweetheart."

Alaine opens the door cautiously, careful not to get too close to the old man. "Did you know him?" she asks.

"Yes, I knew him, unfortunately, and I can tell you a lot about Charles Lindbergh, but it is nothing like what your teacher told you. He was a no good, anti-Semitic, Nazi bastard."

Alaine is shocked by his language, but more curious than ever to know more. "Please tell me why you feel that way."

"Alaine, please sit, this might take a while." She grabs a chair, still careful not to sit to close. "I have not always been a poor, dirty, old man. I have had quite a life, some good, often bad, but always interesting. Listen up."

CHAPTER 2

June 1919

"Chuck, bring that pile of metal over there against the wall and dump it into the wagon," Isaac Levine orders his son. He is the only person who calls him by that name. Charles Albert Levine, now at age 22, has grown into a handsome, stocky man at almost six feet tall and 180 pounds. He has worked at his father's scrap metal company in North Adams, Massachusetts, a small town near Boston, since the age of sixteen, when he dropped out of school reluctantly at his father's insistence. Although healthy, he was unable to serve in the military during WW1 due to bad eyesight.

"Dad, I'm getting tired of you always bossing me around. You seem to give all the orders and I do all the work. And you pay me half of what I deserve."

Isaac Levine is a hard-driving, ambitious man determined to rise above his status as a poor Jewish immigrant from Russia. He is also mean-spirited, cheap, and demanding. "That is the way it is going to be for as long as you work for me."

"I don't know how much longer that will continue," Charles shouts back, as he lifts another heavy load of metal.

Isaac continues to harass his son, "Be careful how you talk to me. Even if you are my son, I can replace you with any half-wit."

For the next two hours, Isaac shouts out orders, and Charles dutifully obeys, his temperature rising with each load of metal he lifts. After one particularly heavy load, Charles throws down his apron and work gloves. "That's it for me today. I must go---I am meeting a friend for dinner."

"It's only 3:30, you have only filled half the wagon."

"Go get another half-wit to finish the job."

Charles hurriedly leaves the garage and rushes home to shower and change. He is meeting his friend in Boston, and he has a long trip in front of him.

Warren Tavern in Boston is one of the oldest taverns in the city if not the entire country, having opened in the mid-1700s. Located near the site of the Battle of Bunker Hill, it is named after Dr. Joseph Warren, one of the early leaders of the Sons of Liberty during Revolutionary times. Patrons at that time included Paul

Revere, Benjamin Franklin, and George Washington. In 1919 it is one of Boston's most popular restaurants, catering to celebrities, political figures, and sports stars. It is a majestic place to dine, exhibiting old-world charm with its dark wood paneling, exquisite antique lighting fixtures, a long mahogany bar, and historically correct low ceilings. And the food isn't half bad.

Charles Levine arrives at Warren Tavern for his dinner reservation at about 8 p.m. His good friend has yet to arrive. The maître d' eyes Charles judgmentally as he enters the establishment. "Mr. Levine, we have a table in the rear near the kitchen for you. Please wait at the bar for your dining companion to arrive."

Charles is accustomed to the prejudicial and disrespectful treatment that Jews are regularly subjected to, but he loudly voices his displeasure. "That is unacceptable, I requested a table near the front."

"Sir, those tables are reserved for our most distinguished guests. You certainly do not fit that description." Charles wants to continue the debate but thinks twice about it. He slowly walks to the bar, confident that the seating arrangement will soon be changing more to his liking.

Ten minutes later a large man enters through the front door. All eyes in the tavern turn to stare at this imposing figure. "Mr. Ruth, so glad you can join us this evening. I have our best table available for you," the maître d' says, fawning over the new arrival.

"That will be just fine," Mr. Ruth bellows in his customary loud voice. "Is Mr. Levine here yet? He will be joining me."

"Yes, he is. He is sitting at the bar. I will go fetch him." The maître d' sheepishly approaches Charles. "I'm sorry for the confusion. Your table in the front is ready for you."

Politely, but sarcastically, Charles responds, "I thought you would see it my way."

George Herman "Babe" Ruth is the most famous and beloved figure in all of Boston. His feats on the baseball field are unsurpassed. His pitching and hitting have led the Boston Red Sox to be The World Series Champions in three out of the last four years. His records, to date, include most home runs in the season of 1918 and consecutive scoreless innings pitched in the World Series from 1916 to 1918. And tonight, he is having dinner with Charles Levine.

Charles has been an avid baseball fan since the age of ten. As is the case with many kids his age, in the New England area, he worships the Boston Red Sox. When *The Babe* joins the team as a rookie in 1914,

Charles writes to him every day. One day, Babe visits North Adams and meets his number one fan. Eventually, they forge a friendship that grows stronger every year as *The Babe* develops into a star.

"So, Babe, how was your day?" Charles asks as they sit down.

"Only ordinary. I pitched seven innings of two-hit, shutout ball, and hit a double and a long home run. We beat those damn Yankees 6 to 0."

"Only ordinary, huh? You're too modest."

Babe laughs loudly. "No one has ever accused me of that."

"Babe, you pitch, and you hit. No one else can do that at your level. Which do you prefer?"

"I think my future is as a hitter. There is no greater thrill than to see that ball sail through the air and land in the stands. The resulting applause gives me such an unbelievable high. Plus, I want to play every day, not just every fourth day as most pitchers do. I am looking forward to hitting home runs for the Red Sox for many years to come.

But enough about me. You can read all that stuff in the newspapers. Tell me, how are you getting on?"

Charles hesitates. In the presence of this most successful man, it is difficult to describe a life going nowhere. "I had another fight with my father. I will never get ahead if I keep working for him."

"Nor should you. If you don't mind me being frank with you, you are too smart to be pushing scrap metal all day. You should be out on your own."

"That's easy for you to say. You have great skills."

"You think pitching and hitting a baseball is easy. I work my tail off every day. As you well know, I came from nowhere, growing up in an orphanage in Baltimore because I was a delinquent. My father did not know how to discipline me, and my mother died when I was only twelve. At the orphanage, everybody picked on me because I was fat and rebellious. But I was determined to succeed. Yes, I had skills, but more than that I had ambition. I wanted to be the best baseball player ever."

Charles listens carefully to what his friend is saying as he sips a beer. With his dominating father, he has always shied away from inserting himself into a leadership role. Babe is a true friend, trying to inspire him to reach higher goals. "Babe, you make a lot of sense. I might not be a baseball star, but you are right I can be better than I am. Confidence, ambition, and the guts to take chances is all I need. I am going to take your words to heart."

"That's my boy. I know you have it in you. Now let's eat."

The Babe is well known for eating prodigious amounts of food. He devours two sixteen-ounce steaks and finishes it off with a pitcher of Sam Adams beer. His reputation is accurate.

As they leave the table, Charles pats the big man on his broad shoulders. "Babe, I want to thank you for this little talk. I now know what I must do."

The next day Charles quits his job with his father.

****

Alaine looks at Charles, confused. "Grandpa, all that you are telling me is interesting, but what does it have to do with Charles Lindbergh?"

"Alaine dear, you need to know my background to truly understand me as a man and what my future holds. I will get to that snake in due time. But now it is dinner time. Go downstairs and eat with your parents. I won't be joining you---these old legs can't handle going up and down the stairs. Afterward, we will continue our little chat."

Alaine hops down the stairs and into the kitchen. Edith has prepared her favorite meal of meatloaf and mashed potatoes. "Mom everything looks scrumptious," says Alaine as she sits down at the table. "Are you aware that Grandpa was friends with Babe Ruth?"

Alaine's father, Philip, laughs. "Did he tell you that? Grandpa Charles has a habit of embellishing his stories."

"What does embellish mean?" Alaine asks.

"It means he tends to exaggerate or even lie. His memory, at his age, can be faulty. I think on purpose."

Edith is quick to defend her father. "That's not fair. I heard some of the same stories before, and I have told you about them. I believed them then, and I believe them now. Phil, you have no proof that Charles did not experience all his friendships and adventures."

"That is true, but I have strong doubts. Alaine, I do not want to dissuade you from listening to your grandpa. If nothing else his stories are captivating, even if they are not true."

"Thanks, Dad. I am looking forward to hearing more."

Alaine gobbles down her dinner. "Mom, can I be excused? I'll bring Grandpa's dinner up to him."

"Go child, I'm sure he appreciates your company."

Charles is groggy, once again napping, as Alaine enters his room. "Who's there?" he asks.

"It's me, Alaine. I have your dinner, and you were telling me about your life."

"Oh yes, those details I never forget. Let me take a few bites and I will continue my story."

CHAPTER 3

January 1920--December 1924

Things have changed quickly in the country since the end of 1919: Prohibition of the sale and consumption of alcohol has been enacted, Babe Ruth has been traded to the hated Yankees, and The Roaring 20's are now in full swing.

Charles Levine has also experienced many changes. After leaving the employ of his father, he moves to Boston and rents a small apartment off Commonwealth Ave. He attends economic classes at nearby Boston University where he learns the nuances of supply and demand. He is determined to become a successful businessman.

One day, while studying in the school's library, a young co-ed approaches him. "Is this seat available?" she asks, pointing to the chair closest to him.

"I think you can see, it is, but I would like my privacy," Charles answers.

Undaunted, the woman plops herself down in the chair in question. "I like this one," she says and then adds,

"My name is Grace Nova, it's nice to meet you." She holds out her hand in a fruitless attempt to shake his. Charles, still bothered by her intrusion, tries to ignore her.

Grace is an aggressive woman, who will not shy away from a confrontation. She is small in stature at only 5' 1" tall and has always struggled with her weight. Her friends describe her appearance and personality as being like a "fireplug".

"I have seen you in my Ecco 101 class. You are the smartest person in the class, but aren't you a little old to be a college freshman?"

Charles can see there is no way to avoid this conversation. He puts out his hand, "Hi Grace, my name is Charles Levine. To resolve your curiosity, I am not an enrolled student—I am just taking a few business classes to further my goals."

"Which would be what?"

"I hope to start a business and make a lot of money."

"Charles, I think we are going to become fast friends—we have a lot in common. What are you doing for dinner tonight?"

The courtship of Charles and Grace is quick. After dating for only three months, Grace is insistent. "If we are going to continue this romance, I must have a ring on my finger, and we should set a date for our wedding."

Charles cannot refuse. He is not exactly sure if it is love that motivates him or the expectation that a successful man needs a strong, intelligent woman by his side. Without hesitation, he answers, "How about next Saturday?"

In a small ceremony, Charles and Grace marry. Grace's parents and her brother are the only attendees.

That evening in bed, after passionate lovemaking, the newlyweds discuss their future. "Ok, I can cross marriage off of my things-to-do list. Now we must figure out how we are going to make a lot of money," Grace says.

"Can I have at least a day of not worrying about that?" replies Charles.

Since arriving in Boston, Charles has held a variety of jobs, none with any future. He has been a waiter, a shoe salesman, and his most enjoyable one, a hotdog vendor at Fenway Park.

Shortly after his marriage, Charles sees a small advertisement in The Boston Globe. A large amount of brass shell casings from the military are for sale. The purchase and recycling of surplus brass shell casings from World War One might not seem like a business where a lot of money can be made. But, on a whim, he answers the ad.

"$3000 for shell casings? Are you crazy? You don't have $3000," his new wife yells at him after he proposes the purchase.

"But your brother does."

Grace's brother is a successful women's dress manufacturer in New York City. Charles negotiates a loan from him, and he finalizes the purchase of the surplus brass.

"Ok, now that you have all this brass, what are you going to do with it?" Grace asks.

"Brass is a very useful component in furniture, art, jewelry, cars, and construction," he answers. "Because of its durability, strength, and attractiveness, it is popular as a vital ingredient in many end-use products."

"I hope you're right."

It turns out, Charles is absolutely right. In a friend's garage, he melts down his initial purchase of the casings, and sells the resulting material, almost overnight, to a local lamp designer. With his profit, he pays off his brother-in-law's loan and buys more casings. He finds out the lessons he learned at the university are on point. The supply of brass is very limited, and the demand is great. His sales continue to grow with little resistance to the price he charges. His margins are impressive.

With the help of a bank loan, he buys a warehouse and builds a manufacturing plant to smelt copper and zinc to form brass. The orders keep flowing in. He incorporates his company under the name, Brass Balls, Inc. The company's rise is rapid--within two years, it is the most dominant supplier of brass in all of New England.

But it is not enough for Charles and Grace—they both want more. With the need for more capital, the company goes public with a successful initial public offering. Charles is its largest stockholder. With the additional funds in place, they expand by opening new plants in Pennsylvania, Maryland, and Michigan.

In Detroit, the automobile manufacturing business is exploding. General Motors, Chrysler, and Chevrolet have tremendous demand for their cars. A key component in these cars is brass, causing the automobile companies to become Brass Balls' largest customers. The company soon becomes the largest supplier of brass in the entire country.

One company Charles will not sell to is The Ford Motor Company, because of its founder and chairman, Henry Ford.

Antisemitism has become rampant in the United States and all over the world. The prejudice Jews and Jewish businesses face every day is appalling and dangerous. With his success, Charles feels he must take the responsibility of speaking out. He needs to do his share to combat this hate speech in any way he can.

"Henry Ford is the most prominent antisemite in the country," Charles tells his general manager. "In an article in his newspaper, The Dearborn Chronicle, Ford writes that Jews are *The World's Foremost Problem.* I will not have that horrible man benefit from our products."

The profits from Brass Balls keep rolling in and within five years, Charles becomes a millionaire, many times over. His family is expanding also. Grace gives birth to a daughter, Eloise, in December of 1920 followed by another daughter, Ardith, in February 1924.

Charles turns out to be a very good father. He regularly plays with his children, celebrates their birthdays with huge parties, and showers them with toys and other gifts. He also oversees their upbringing and insists on them receiving the best education possible.

With their newfound wealth and larger family, he and Grace move into a large mansion on Beacon Hill, the ritziest section of Boston. They entertain lavishly and go to all the most important gatherings. In addition, they both become leaders in important Jewish causes.

Grace becomes comfortable living the good life. She is content with her surroundings, belongings, and numerous luxuries. After one extravagant party, she proclaims to Charles, "I think we can now rest on our laurels. It is time for us to relax and travel the world."

Charles is of another mindset. He is not satisfied with his achievements. "There will be no laurel resting in this family. I need other mountains to climb."

CHAPTER 4

January 1925

A young woman is giving a speech at M.I.T. in Boston. She has recently gained fame through a series of newspaper articles she has written about her experiences in aviation including her record-breaking flight by a woman of 14,000 feet high. Charles decides to attend the lecture. The woman's name is Amelia Earhart.

Charles is immediately enthralled by her speech. For the next hour and a half, he is transfixed by her thoughts on aviation.

"It is the wave of the future, and in the coming years it will become the most significant means of travel around the country and the world," Amelia announces.

"Flights will be able to take passengers to the next city or entirely cross country in a fraction of the time it would take a car or train. Bigger, better, and faster airplanes will be built. Safety issues will be allayed to the point of little or no concern. Large airports will spring up everywhere. And people who invest in this new industry will make a lot of money."

Charles is smitten by her perky good looks, charismatic personality, and her enthusiasm for the subject. Although he is a married man, Charles does have a wandering eye.

After the lecture, Charles boldly approaches the podium. "Miss Earhart, I would like to know more about aviation. Would you accompany me for dinner tonight to discuss your experiences and my possible involvement?"

Amelia repels his advances. She is accustomed to suspicious invitations from men. "No, I am sorry. Dinner is out of the question, but I will join you for a cup of coffee in the lounge across the hall."

Delighted to be able to have more time with this special person, Charles readily agrees. "That will be wonderful."

Charles gives a quick summary of his background and successes to Amelia. She is impressed. "You are obviously a successful man. Are you serious about your interest in aviation?"

"Up until now, I have not given it much thought, but your speech has inspired me. I am always looking for new adventures. How do I break into this field?"

22

"With your financial abilities, it will not be difficult. Money goes a long way in opening doors. I will be glad to introduce you to the right people to get you started."

"That is much appreciated." As they leave the lounge, Charles asks one last question. "Are you ever afraid?"

"Never," she quickly responds. "I always look forward to every flight, confident that I will return safely."

****

Alaine grows impatient. The subject of her desire has not even been mentioned in the long hours of Charles' storytelling. "Charles Lindbergh, remember him? When does his name come up?"

Charles attempts to soothe her anxiousness, "Shortly, we will arrive into the world of Mr. Lindbergh. I warn you it will not be pretty. But now it is the hour of my bedtime, and I assume yours too. We will pick this up tomorrow after school."

"Tomorrow is Saturday, there is no school. We can talk in the morning."

Who is Charles Levine?

"All the better."

Part II: THE AVIATOR

CHAPTER 1

May 1925---April 1927

Through an introduction from Amelia, Charles meets Giuseppe Bellanca for lunch at a restaurant on Long Island, NY.

"Hello Giuseppe, I am Charles Levine. It is so nice to meet you. I have heard such great things about you from Amelia."

In a thick Italian accent, Giuseppe replies, "She is too kind. I've had my ups and downs."

"From what I have learned about you, it has been mostly ups."

Giuseppe is a renowned airplane designer. He is an Italian immigrant who in 1913 pioneered plane safety and performance by making radical changes to airplane construction. He moved the propeller to the front, the wing

25

to the middle, and the tail to the rear. Instantly it becomes the new standard in the industry. In 1922 he builds the first plane with an enclosed cabin. It is a brilliant revelation in design.

However, by 1925, he has fallen on hard times. Many of his newer designs are failures. However, he still has the utmost confidence in his ability to design and build superlative airplanes.

After the first course is served, Charles asks, "You don't mind if I call you Joe? That is the Anglo interpretation of your name?"

"No, please do-- everyone does. Now tell me about yourself. I understand you are quite successful."

"I started a small company about five years ago, and it blossomed into a very profitable one. I was lucky."

"I am sure it was more than luck. Your intelligence and hard work certainly had a lot to do with your achievements."

"Yes, I guess that is true, thank you."

"Now you want to get into aviation. Why is that?"

"It's the future, and I want to be a part of it. I am hoping you are the right person who can take me there."

"Building aircraft is an expensive endeavor. I have been burdened by a lack of funds."

"That is where I can help. I'm prepared to invest in whatever is needed. What is your goal?"

"I want to design the best airplane in the world and win *The Orteig Prize*."

Raymond Orteig is the owner of a New York hotel. He desires to provide stimulus to the aviation industry by proposing a prize of $25,000 in 1919 to the first person or persons from a World War One Allied Country to fly across the Atlantic Ocean in a non-stop flight from New York to Paris. By 1926, no one has been able to claim *The Orteig Prize*. All who have tried have failed, resulting in many deaths. The consensus is that this perilous journey is too difficult for the current state of aviation.

"I have been told that the trip cannot be done. In fact, no one has even tried in the last two years," says Charles.

"It can be done," says Joe.

"Your confidence has made me a believer. I want in. Together we can make it happen."

The two men talk for hours, each describing their views on a partnership. They see eye to eye. Charles will provide the necessary funds, and Joe the expertise. Their only objective is to design, build, and fly the best aircraft of its time---a plane that can successfully fly across the Atlantic Ocean and capture *The Orteig Prize.* Charles and Joe shake hands. Their new company will be the Columbia Aircraft Corporation, based at Roosevelt Field on Long Island N.Y.

Over the next few months, Joe uses his considerable skills to finish the design of *The Columbia.* Its major advantage will be its ability to lift twice the weight of the other aircraft of the time. This will enable it to carry enough fuel to make long-range flights.

After the design is completed, the next step is the plane's construction. Joe hires the best mechanics available and arduously supervises every detail. It is a laborious process. Charles fulfills his obligation by paying the bills.

In surprisingly quick fashion *The Columbia* is built and ready for a test flight. Joe, Charles, and the whole crew watch as their creation soars into flight for the first time without a flaw. In the following weeks, further tests are scheduled. The *Columbia* passes all tests with "flying colors."

"Are we ready?" Charles asks Joe in early April 1927.

Always confident, Joe replies, "Yes, we are."

Only one question remains. Who is going to be the lead pilot? They both think of the same person, a young, cocky man by the name of Charles Augustes Lindbergh.

Charles A. Lindbergh is born on February 4, 1902, in Detroit, Michigan, and moves to Little Falls, Minnesota at an early age. His parents are Charles, a U.S. Congressman, and Evangeline, a teacher. His father is one of the only congressmen to oppose the U.S. entry into World War I, a foreshadowing of his son's stance before the U.S. entry into World War II. Charles in adulthood is tall, handsome, and full of confidence.

Charles becomes interested in aviation at the age of 19 when he takes his first flying lesson. He soon is deeply immersed in the industry: first, as a daredevil in barnstorming tours and then as a military pilot in the U.S. Army Air Service. He eventually becomes a second lieutenant in the Air Service Reserve Corps. He is considered bright, ambitious, and adventurous. These traits, in 1927, bring him to New York on a quest for glory to capture *The Orteig Prize.*

Roosevelt Field is a large airfield near Mineola, Long Island, NY. During WW I, it was used for training, and after the war, it is named in honor of Theodore

Roosevelt's son, Quentin, who was killed in combat. By 1927, it has become America's busiest civilian airfield. Because of its long runway of 5,000 feet and its most eastern location, it is the preferred airfield for any proposed flight to Europe. It is here in April that the two Charles' have picked for their first meeting. The meeting does not go well.

"I understand you are the Jew who is funding the building of Joe Bellanca's plane," Lindbergh abrasively bellows.

Charles Levine is taken aback by Lindbergh's obvious antisemitic taunt, but he does not show it. "Yes, Joe and I built *The Columbia.* It is the best aircraft in the world. We are very proud of it. I understand you might be interested in piloting it across The Atlantic."

Lindbergh answers smugly, "That remains to be seen; I am keeping my options open. You do know I am the best damn pilot here. Other designers are interested in my services."

Levine is offended by the man. His contempt for him grows with each word out of his mouth. "Mr. Lindbergh, your qualifications as a pilot are impressive, but we are also looking for a man with character and dignity."

Now it is Lindbergh's turn to be taken aback, "Are you saying I am not good enough for your Jew plane?"

Charles Levine wants to kick the bastard in the butt but controls himself. In deference to his partner, he does not say what is truly on his mind.

"Mr. Lindbergh, we have just met, please allow me some time to make an informed decision on who we will allow to guide our plane. Good day, Mr. Lindbergh, we will get back to you shortly." The two men walk away without shaking hands.

Charles Levine and Joe Bellanca meet at a small speakeasy to have a cocktail and discuss their options. Although Prohibition is still in effect, all who want to drink are able, if they know the right places to go. Charles is furious. "Lindbergh is an egotistical, selfish anti-Semite. I will not have him flying our plane."

Joe responds calmly, "I understand your feelings, his personality is in question, but he certainly knows his stuff."

"Anybody with rudimentary skills can fly our plane. We have built in all the safeguards needed to assure our success."

"You are making light of what is needed to pilot a plane that far over dangerous seas. I am not worried about our plane, but I am concerned about the possibility of pilot error. We need a man who has ambition, endurance, and the strong will to overcome any obstacle he may encounter. Charles Lindbergh is such a man."

Charles takes another drink, a double this time. "He is still an asshole!"

"Charles, we must stop arguing. I will meet with the man alone. I promise you if I find any evidence of a difficult attitude, we will go in another direction."

"I have no doubt you will see it my way."

Joe Bellanca and Charles Lindbergh meet for lunch in a diner in Garden City. Lindbergh starts the conversation poorly. "Joe, how did a good Christian like yourself end up with a money-hungry Jew as a partner?"

"Charles, let's leave religion out of this. This is a serious matter—do you want to fly our airplane or not?"

"I am considering it, but I have a few conditions."

It does not take Joe long to understand what his partner has been saying. "Conditions? What conditions are you talking about?"

"I understand *The Columbia* is a two-seater with room for a lead pilot and a co-pilot/passenger. Is that correct?"

"Yes, quite so. That is the best way to attempt to fly a long distance. The lead pilot, the captain, will steer the aircraft most of the time, with the co-pilot substituting when necessary to give the captain a rest. For the approximately 35 hours they will be in the air, that is the safest method. Of course, we are considering you to be the lead pilot."

"That is unacceptable to me. I insist on going solo on that flight. My reputation is at stake. I don't want an incompetent to screw up my chance of succeeding."

Joe has heard enough. "You are being foolish. On such a long flight you are bound to get tired. You and the plane will crash if you fall asleep at the controls."

Lindbergh will not back down. "I will not fall asleep. You have heard my demand—take it or leave it."

"We will leave it. I will not take the risks you are suggesting." Joe takes the last bite of his sandwich and leaves the table abruptly. As he does so, he politely says, "I wish you good day and good luck."

Lindbergh yells out when Joe is five feet away, "We will see who has the good luck."

Later that day, Joe and Charles Levine talk. "You are right—that man is an asshole," says Joe. "He selfishly wants individual glory and publicity at the price of safety. We do not need him."

Charles smiles at Joe's decision. "Thank you for seeing it my way. We can find another man for the job, and I have just the right person in mind—me."

Joe stares at Charles—speechless.

****

Alaine is overjoyed. The mention of Charles Lindbergh's name has renewed her interest in Charles' stories. "You are right Grandpa; Charles Lindbergh does not sound like a very nice man."

"You have heard nothing so far, the worst about him is yet to come."

CHAPTER 2

May 1927

Joe calls Grace, Charles' wife, in Boston. "He wants to pilot *The Columbia* across The Atlantic himself," he yells into the phone.

"Is he crazy? He can't do that. I'm catching the next train to New York. I will be there tomorrow."

Charles has recently taken several flying lessons, and according to his instructor, he has done fairly well. But his instructor, Joe, and Grace all agree that he is far too inexperienced to attempt such a difficult flight. Now they must convince Charles.

Grace grabs a taxicab from Grand Central Station and heads immediately to Roosevelt Field, where Charles is making an inspection of *The Columbia.* "You are not piloting that plane", are the first words out of her mouth.

Charles is surprised by her appearance and her greeting. "Hello darling, it's nice to see you too."

She makes her case quickly, "Men who actually know how to fly have died trying." As is often the case, she is infuriated by his reckless behavior. "You will not make me a widow now."

"You are being overly dramatic. I know I can do this. Our plane is the safest ever."

"You are not listening to what I am trying to say. You cannot risk death now—we are going to have another child."

Charles stands silent for a moment; Grace's surprise announcement makes him think. He runs to his wife. "Oh my God, this is wonderful. How long have you known?"

"About three months---I did not want to disturb you while you were working so hard on your project. But under the circumstances, you must now know why I feel so strongly."

"Of course, you are right. I still think you are being unnecessarily fearful, but I will not be the lead pilot of *The Columbia.*" Charles, however, does not say what is now on his mind.

While the Bellanca/Levine team has been scrambling to find a captain, Charles Lindbergh has not been sitting idly by. In February, The Ryan Aircraft Corp. of San Diego starts construction on a small single-engine plane, financed by two businessmen from St. Louis, and designed by Donald Hall. The plane's name is *The Spirit of St. Louis.* By May it should be ready for flight and an attempt at *The Orteig Prize.*

After Lindbergh's unsuccessful partnership with Bellanca/Levine, he agrees with The Ryan Company and Hall to be their pilot. The plane has room only for one person, keeping with Lindbergh's demands. Both teams pick Roosevelt Field in New York as their taking-off point.

It is now readily apparent that a race is in effect between *The Spirit of St. Louis* and *The Columbia* to see which team will be first to take off for the transatlantic flight to Paris.

"I have just learned that Lindbergh will be piloting *The Spirit of St. Louis,*" Charles says to Joe.

"And I have learned from their chief mechanic that it can be as long as a month before they are ready for flight," says Joe.

"We can beat them."

"There remains only one small problem—we still need pilots!"

After his dalliance with Lindbergh and listening to Charles' foolhardy idea, Joe meets with Lloyd Bertaud and Clarence Chamberlin. Bertaud is an experienced pilot from World War I where he was a lieutenant in the U.S. Army Air Services. Chamberlin is well-known as a pilot with an excellent reputation. His main claim to fame is his record for endurance. He recently set a record by staying in the air for over 45 hours. Fearful they will soon find other jobs, Joe hires both of them, without telling Charles. Chamberlin will be the captain and lead pilot and Bertaud will be the co-pilot and navigator.

"You hired who?" Charles is livid when he finds out what Joe has done. "I must object."

"Charles, we have been searching for pilots for weeks. These two men are vastly qualified. I did not want to waste any more time."

"I have no problem with Chamberlin; he is an excellent pilot, but Bertaud has to go."

"Why?"

"Because I am going to be the co-pilot."

"We have been through this before. You agreed with Grace and me that you would not do that."

"What I agreed to is that I would not be the lead pilot and captain. Grace's concern is that I am too inexperienced to guide the plane to Paris. She is right. My inexperience could lead to problems due to pilot error. Now we have a pilot with vast experience. With me as co-pilot the risks are minimal."

"You are making our flight sound easy. You know that is not the case. However, I am not going to argue with you any longer, but you have to tell Grace and Bertaud."

Charles dreads both conversations. First up is his wife. He waits until that evening when he is cuddled up with her in bed at the Garden City Hotel. "Honey, I must tell you something. I am going to be the co-pilot on our flight to Paris."

Grace is in no mood for this argument. "You are not—we have already discussed this."

"What we discussed was my role as the lead pilot. That is not to be the case. I am going to be the co-pilot."

"What is the difference? You are putting yourself at risk for a stupid prize."

"I am not doing this for the $25,000. It is going to be an accomplishment the whole world will be talking about. It will bring fame for us and respect for the Jewish faith."

Grace is not buying into his reasoning. They argue for hours. "Charles you are a fool. I see I cannot dissuade you from your idiotic plans. I am going back to Boston tomorrow. I will not watch you die." She turns her back to him and goes to sleep.

Charles finds Bertaud in the hanger looking over the aircraft. Charles walks over to him with his head down, "Lloyd come here and sit down. I have some bad news."

"What is it?" Lloyd asks, "Is there something wrong with the plane?"

"No, the plane is fine," Charles says softly. "We are replacing you as co-pilot."

Lloyd raises his voice, "You are doing what?"

"I'm sorry, you heard me right, you are no longer flying to Paris."

Lloyd's anger is clear. "And who is replacing me?"

"I am."

"You? You have no skills."

"My skill is that I own the plane."

Lloyd stands up and yells, "I will fight you on this. Your partner committed to me."

"Please calm down. I am uncommitting—there is nothing in writing. You cannot change my mind on this decision."

"We will see about that. You have not heard the last from me." Lloyd walks briskly out of the hangar. At that moment, Joe walks in. The two men pass each other without saying a word.

Joe stops to talk to Charles, "I assume that did not go well."

"You assume right, but now let's move on. The plane is ready, our pilots are set, and the forecast is good. We can schedule our takeoff for three days hence on May 19."

"Sounds good to me," Joe cheerfully agrees.

Charles and Joe's happiness seems secure. What could go wrong? Unfortunately for them and their plans for glory, the answer is plenty.

The word spreads quickly throughout Roosevelt Field—Chamberlin is in as the lead pilot, Bertaud is out, Levine is in as the co-pilot, and *The Columbia* is ready to go.

Charles Lindbergh visits with Bertaud to commiserate. They are old friends from years of friendly competition in aviation events. "You can't let them get away with this," says Lindbergh. "Levine's behavior is abhorrent, but not surprising. It is to be expected from his kind."

"I agree, but what can I do?" asks Bertaud.

For his selfish reasons, Lindbergh is anxious to help. "I have an idea. I know of a lawyer in New York who I have used on occasion. He is very bright. Maybe he can think of something."

"I am willing to meet with him, but I cannot afford a lawyer."

"Don't let that concern you; I will pay his bill. It's the least I can do to help a good friend."

Bertaud does not question Lindbergh's motives. "Let's go see him."

Robert Larson is a clever attorney, specializing in contract law. Lindbergh and Bertaud apprise him of the situation. He hesitates to speak for a few moments, thinking over his options. "The fact that there is nothing in writing makes this a difficult case. But I am familiar with The Nassau County Civil Court, and I know of a judge there that I think will be favorable to our cause. My thoughts are that in the short term, the best we can do is to get a temporary injunction to hold up their flight for a few days. Does that do you guys any good?"

"That is good for me," says Lindbergh joyfully.

Bertaud is starting to understand why Lindbergh is being so helpful. "How does that help me?"

Larson replies, "Not much, but in the long term, we can sue for damages. It is a long shot, but it might result in a few dollars for you in the future."

Disappointed, Bertaud says, "I guess I will have to be satisfied with that."

Bellanca, Levine, and their mechanics are celebrating at their favorite watering hole. They know they are on the cusp of winning the race to Paris. Their party is interrupted by the appearance of a tall stranger. He hands Charles an official-looking document. "You have been served," he quickly says and turns to walk out of the bar.

Charles reads the papers out loud: *"By the order of Judge Frank Milner of the Nassau Civil Court—We find sufficient evidence due to the dismissal of one Lloyd Bertaud to issue the following temporary injunction order: That the aircraft "The Columbia" shall not be permitted to*

43

fly out of New York for a period of at least seven days starting on this day of May 13, 1927. Furthermore, This Order shall stay in effect until vacated by This Court upon further evidence presented by the parties involved."

"What is this shit?" asks Joe.

Charles is infuriated. "It means that we are fucked, and I smell the rat who is fucking us, his name is Charles Lindbergh."

The emotions caused by this court order are aptly diverse. Bellanca and Levine are crushed, Lindbergh is elated, and Bertaud is indifferent. Joe states the obvious, "This means we cannot take off until the order is lifted which will be May 21, at the earliest."

Lindbergh tells his plane's designer, Hall, "We are taking off early on May 20."

CHAPTER 3

May 1927

"Charles, we are not ready for takeoff. We need another day for final adjustments," says Donald Hall to Lindbergh. "I am the plane's designer, and I know what it is capable of and what would be foolhardy. What difference will a day make?"

"We must fly today. Don't ask me why, just make it so," insists Charles. "It is 6 a.m.; I am leaving no later than 8 a.m."

Not wishing to fight Lindbergh, Hall relents. For the next hour and a half, the crew of *The Spirit of St. Louis* scrambles to prepare the plane for flight. They adjust the struts on the wings, fill the gas tanks to the brim, and check the air pressure of the wheels. Their main objective, however, is to make the weight of the plane as light as possible so that the fuel supply is sufficient for such a long journey. The only way to accomplish that goal safely is to remove contents. Among other items, out goes a two-way radio, a camera, a seat cushion, and even a map. By 7:30 a.m., Hall and his mechanics have finished their remaining tasks.

"Ok Charles, we have eliminated every non-essential ounce. We are now a go."

"Fabulous, I knew you could do it." Charles Lindbergh puts on his helmet and is lifted into his cramped seat. He expertly checks all his controls. "All is in order. Let's roll this baby onto the runway," he yells out.

At 7:52 a.m., May 20, the engines roar and *The Spirit of St. Louis* lifts off on its historic flight to Paris. A smattering of press takes pictures and a large audience of about one thousand witnesses wildly cheer. Charles Lindbergh sits back and smiles smugly.

Meanwhile, not a hundred yards away, *The Columbia* stands silently in its hanger. The court order is lifted at 5 p.m. on May 20, but it is too late. Charles Levine solemnly watches Lindbergh's takeoff, his dream for glory unceremoniously thwarted.

The flight of Charles Lindbergh and *The Spirit of St. Louis,* as is well known, is successful, but not without its moments of anxiety. Within seconds of taking off, Lindbergh faces his first challenge---in front of him at the end of the airfield are low-hanging telephone wires. He clears them only by a few feet.

As he passes over Long Island Sound, Connecticut, and the open seas of the Atlantic Ocean, turbulence causes rapid shifting of altitudes, but the biggest problem, as Joe Bellanca predicted, is tiredness. Prior to taking off, Lindbergh had not slept for 10 hours due to nerves and preparatory details. Now, only two hours into the flight, he becomes drowsy. It is a condition he will suffer for the entire flight. To fight his fatigue, he decides to attempt a maneuver—he descends to only ten feet above the water. It is a dangerous and foolish endeavor, but it is successful--he pulls up at the last moment, barely avoiding a crash into the ocean below.

It is smooth sailing for the rest of the daylight hours, but as the night sky approaches, fog moves in, and visibility suffers. Lindbergh climbs to 10,000 feet to avoid the low-hanging clouds—it is a mistake. Ice forms on the wings and the aircraft behaves erratically. Lindbergh is not thinking clearly, and he starts talking to himself. *"Yeah, I am tired as hell, but I must stop making these stupid errors."* He lowers the plane to warmer air temperatures at 7000 feet.

Seventeen hours into the flight, he is halfway home to his goal, but danger still lies ahead. It is now twenty-seven hours since he has had any sleep and its effects have worsened. He falls asleep! Luckily as the plane descends rapidly, he wakes up to pull the plane level.

Lindbergh continues to doze off and hallucinate through the rest of the flight, but his determination and skills overcome the perils.

After flying for over twenty-eight hours, Lindbergh spots the coast of Ireland. He has reached Europe.

Word has spread quickly throughout Paris of the impending arrival of *The Spirit of St. Louis* and its great American pilot. A throng of over 100,000 people converge at the airport to be a part of this historic event. Five hours after flying past Ireland and England he lands at Le Bourget Aerodrome in Paris at 5:22 p.m. New York time, May 21.

A crowd rush to the cockpit, lift Lindbergh upon their shoulders, and parade him around the field in an unprecedented congratulatory celebration.

The next day, after a night of much-needed sleep, he meets with dignitaries, both American and French to accept their overwhelming acclaim, as well as the prize money of $25,000. Newspaper and radio reports from around the world hail him as a conquering hero and even as a God among men.

Weeks later, when he returns to the United States, even more accolades are bestowed on him. In New York, a ticker-tape parade through the Canyon of Heroes is held in his honor. In Washington, President Calvin Coolidge, awards him The Distinguished Flying Cross and the Medal of Honor, even though their intended purpose is only for combat bravery. A postal stamp in his honor is issued, and Time magazine names him their first *Man of the Year.*

Charles Levine, Joe Bellanca, and the rest of the crew of *The Columbia* bemoan in disbelief at the quantity and quality of the awards and acclaim. They know this man---he is no hero.

****

"Grandpa, that could have been you receiving all that fame," Alaine astutely says.

"It not only could have been—it should have been, except for duplicitous acts of that man."

"I don't know what duplicitous means, but I bet it is bad."

"That would be a very good bet. It means deceptive and meanspirited, and that certainly was him." Charles and Alaine both sigh.

"History would have been a lot different if this Jewish man rather than this fiendish anti-Semite had gotten his chance. It is a bitterness and regret that I suffer with to this day."

Alaine puts her arm around Charles and kisses him on the top of his head. Consoling him as best she can, "Please let's move on," she kindly says. "I'm sure you have other stories to tell."

"Yes, I do. Unfortunately, much of the worst still revolves around Lindbergh. But those stories will have to wait for another day. First, let me tell you about my day in the sun."

CHAPTER 4

June 1927

Charles Levine does not let the disappointment of losing out on *The Orteig Prize* and the resulting fame from it keep him down for long. He is determined to attempt another challenging goal.

Two days after Lindbergh lands in Paris, an international group offers a prize of $15,000 for an aircraft to fly transatlantic from America to Germany. It will be a flight 300 miles, nine hours longer, and much more dangerous than what Lindbergh has accomplished. In addition, it is stipulated that a passenger must be aboard. Levine, Bellanca, and Chamberlin have no doubts that *The Columbia* will be up to the challenge.

To gain added publicity, Levine decides to have a little fun with the newspapermen covering the story. He announces to them, "Clarence Chamberlin will be the lead pilot, but the passenger will, as of now, remain a mystery. I will let all of you wise men and women speculate on who it will be."

The mystery arouses much interest in the flight. Proposed names include all sorts of celebrities, sports stars, and politicians. Some of the names mentioned are Amelia Earhart, actress Greta Garbo, tennis great, Bill Tilden, and even President Coolidge. Joe Bellanca does not even know the identity of the passenger.

On June 4, *The Columbia* is ready to go. Chamberlin directs the plane onto the runway with the passenger seat still vacant. Charles announces to the large crowd that has assembled, "I will occupy the vacant seat, for the time being while we await the arrival of the mystery passenger. In the interim, we will taxi around the runway."

On the third trip around the airfield, *The Columbia* suddenly picks up speed. It is now clear that the supposed mystery is a ruse—Charles Levine has fooled everybody; he is to be the passenger. *The Columbia* lifts off.

Charles' daughter, Eloise, breaks into tears and yells, "Daddy, what are you doing?"

His wife, Grace, screams out, "Oh no," and immediately faints. That night Grace has a miscarriage and loses her baby boy. Grace will never forgive Charles.

In the air, Charles looks down, waves goodbye, and says, "Next stop—Berlin."

The flight goes without a flaw for about twelve hours until Chamberlin needs a rest. "Charles, I would like to get some shuteye; can you take over the controls for a little while?"

"Sure can," responds Levine. "I have been waiting for this opportunity."

Charles does well initially, but an hour later problems arise due to Levine's lack of experience. The plane rises to a dangerous level, followed by too fast a descent and an adverse yaw. Just before the plane stalls out, Chamberlin awakes. "Charles, what the hell are you doing?" He expertly takes control and levels the plane to a safe altitude. "I think it best if I stay awake for the rest of the flight."

Levine's skills as a navigator prove to be as inept as those of his piloting. He somehow loses his compass and maps, most likely falling out of the plane during his piloting. These losses are costly—they veer widely off course. Chamberlin makes several corrections to head the aircraft in the right direction, but the adjustments result in a dangerous loss of fuel. Arrival in Berlin is now in question. Chamberlin slows the plane to conserve fuel, but his efforts are not enough. The plane lands in a wheatfield only 40 miles short of its target, 43 hours after takeoff from New York. They quickly refuel and land at the

Berlin airport thirty minutes later, where Chamberlin and Levine are enthusiastically acknowledged for surpassing the mileage and speed records of Lindbergh's flight. Levine is hailed as a hero for being the first transatlantic passenger.

In the weeks that follow, the pair receive numerous congratulations and awards from around the world. Their faces are splashed on countless newspapers. Proudly, they are received and honored by Paul Von Hindenburg, the president of Germany, Benito Mussolini, the dictator of Italy, and even The Pope. However, the greatest adulation that Levine receives is bestowed by the Jews of the world. He is widely praised by them for his courage and determination. So proud of his heroism, Jewish songs are even written in his honor.

Charles Levine has attained the glory that he has long sought. But as he will soon find out, fame is fleeting.

****

"Gee Grandpa, you are a real hero. I can't wait to tell my teacher about you on Monday."

"Not so fast kiddo, there is more to hear. It is not always heroic. The next story, for instance, revolves around a woman. But it would be wrong for you to hear it."

"Why?" Alaine asks naively.

"It deals with a subject matter that is inappropriate for a child." Charles thinks over his dilemma. "I have an idea—why don't I tell it to your parents and have them censor out the parts they would not want you to know."

Charles starts to stand up. He struggles to do so. "Please help me get down to the living room and have your parents meet me there."

As they start the arduous descent down the staircase, Alaine yells out, "Mom, Dad, Grandpa wants to talk to you. Come to the living room."

Edith and Philip arrive in the living room just as Alaine and Charles strive to get there also. Charles plops himself onto the old, frayed recliner as Philip begins to speak, "Ok we're here, what is it you want to say?"

Charles responds in a low, hoarse voice, "There is a delicate portion of my life that I want to address, but Alaine is a little too young to hear it. I think it best to tell it to you first."

"From my point of view, she is a little young to hear anything you have to say, and I'm not sure I want to hear it either," says Philip.

From the first, Alaine's father was against bringing Charles into their home to live. It is his opinion that the old man is a bullshit artist and con man. He does not want fanciful tales to negatively influence his impressionable daughter.

Edith disagrees with her husband, "Phil, it is true that my father has had an erratic life, however, I see no harm in him relating adventures which I believe are mostly true."

Philip raises his voice, "The keyword there is *mostly*. Alaine, you must realize that a lot of what Charles is telling you comes from his warped imagination."

Charles interrupts his son-in-law, "Phil, I take issue with your comments. Yes, maybe, my memory is not perfect, but the gist of what I have told her is accurate."

"I strongly doubt that," Phil shouts out.

Alaine has heard enough, "Mom, Dad, Grandpa, please stop your bickering; it is very disturbing. I'm going to my room."

Edith tries to clear the air. "Phil, please give my Dad a chance to say his piece."

"Ok, I will—but I remain dubious."

Charles is confused; he is not sure how to begin. After a moment to collect his thoughts, he suddenly bursts out, "I could not help myself—the woman was so damn gorgeous."

CHAPTER 5

June-July, 1927

As soon as Charles Levine steps out of the plane in Berlin after his historic flight, he is embraced by a ravishing woman with a big hug and kiss.

Charles is startled by this surprising show of affection. He pries himself loose from her arms. "Do I know you?" he asks.

The woman is offended. "You very well should. I am the famous Mabel Boll."

Mabel Boll is well known in the United States as Broadway's most beautiful actress and singer and, in New York, as one of its most prominent socialites. She has golden blond hair, warm brown eyes, and an exquisite figure. In the language of the times, she is an *it girl*, known for a personality and sex appeal that is especially engaging.

"Mr. Levine, I am your biggest admirer." Mabel is quick to show off her voluminous body with many diamond necklaces hanging from it.

Charles is impressed and aroused. He grabs her hand, and provokingly responds, "Please call me Charles."

She smiles, "I would love to get to know you better. Can you join me for dinner tonight?"

Charles is tired from his long trip. He would prefer to have a quick meal and go right to bed, but he can't refuse this tempting invitation. "Yes, of course, it will be my pleasure."

After dinner, the newly formed couple remove to her suite at the best hotel in Berlin. There they spend a long, enjoyable night of ravenous lovemaking.

"I think this evening is going to be the best reward I am going to receive," Charles says.

"Darling, this is only the first of many prizes I will be giving you."

Mabel is married to Hernando Rocha, a wealthy coffee magnate. Charles, of course, is still married to Grace. But these facts do not prevent them from starting a torrid love affair.

Throughout the world, Mabel is known as the *Queen of Diamonds* for the large diamonds she always wears, generous gifts from her husband. Charles is now known as the *King of the Sky,* for his historic journey. For the next month, they parade around Berlin and other

European cities as *The King and his Queen.* They make an imposing and happy couple.

Newspapers in Boston are filled with pictures and accounts of Charles and the magnificent women by his side. Grace sees them all. She confides to her best friend, "I have had enough of that philandering bastard." She files for divorce, and her lawyers prepare a separation agreement.

Charles receives the news of the filing by an urgent telegram. At the time, he is again in bed with Mabel enjoying another long night of sexual adventures.

"Oh shit," he says.

"What's wrong darling?" Mabel asks.

"It's this damn telegram, Grace wants a divorce."

"So, give it to her. I'll get one too, and we'll spend the rest of our lives together, having fun."

"It's not that easy. I have two children, who I love dearly." Charles dreads what he has to say next. "Mabel, I adore you, but we must end our fling now. I must try to reconcile with my wife."

Mabel is accustomed to this type of conversation---this is not her first affair, nor will it be her last. "Sweetheart, I understand. Do what you must. I will move on."

She starts to get dressed. "There is one favor I ask of you before we part ways altogether."

"What might that be?"

"I need you to fly me to America. I want to be the first woman to cross the Atlantic in a plane."

****

"You were right not to tell Alaine this part of your story. I will relay it to her without the sex," says Edith.

"I never heard of Mabel Boll. Was she even real?" asks Philip.

"She was very real. You must remember our affair took place over fifty years ago. Back in the day, Mabel was a big celebrity. Her exploits were legendary. My heart still aches for her."

"She sounds like a slut to me," says Philip.

"Yes, that too," answers Charles with a sly smile.

"I have one last question; did you ever fly Mabel to America?" asks Edith.

"That is a story for another day. Please tell Alaine to see me tomorrow. Now I am going to bed; please help me to my room."

CHAPTER 6

August 1927--June 1928

Chamberlin and Levine fly to Paris in *The Columbia.* It is going to be their first stop before going on to London and then back to America. In Paris, Charles again meets up with Mabel Boll who has taken a train to be there.

"Charles, remember the favor I asked of you in Berlin. Are you now ready to fly me to America?" Mabel is determined to be the first woman to cross the Atlantic. She is convinced that the publicity will enhance her reputation as one of the most preeminent women in the world.

Charles shakes his head. "I don't know if I can find a pilot who will do that," he answers.

Mabel chooses to use her considerable charms to persuade him. She moves closer to him and attempts to place a big kiss on his lips. "Please honey, it is important to me."

Charles fends her off. "Stop, that part of our lives is over. As I said, I need to find a pilot."

Chamberlin refuses, as does a French pilot. "I know of another pilot in London who might do it. The problem is how do I get the plane there?" he explains to Mabel.

"Why don't you fly it there yourself?" she asks.

"Me? I don't think that is a good idea. Flying over the English Chanel is a hazardous trip."

Mabel, at this point, cares little about Charles' safety. She appeals to his ego, "You're selling yourself short. You are a capable pilot. I know you can do it."

Beaming at the compliment, "You're right, I can do it."

"Great." Mabel, not wanting to trust the inexperienced pilot for her own safety, adds, "I'll meet you in London; I am taking a boat."

That night Charles slips into the hangar and starts the engine of *The Columbia.* He is rusty and his attempts for takeoff are problematic. He struggles to attain the necessary speed to get airborne and makes three failed tries before he can finally get the plane in the air. The flight itself is smooth, although he goes off-course twice.

The only thing worse than the takeoff is the landing. He bounces the plane four times before it comes to rest in London, just yards away from a large storage building. "That was scary," he proclaims to the ground attendant who helps him exit the plane.

Two days later Mabel arrives in London, only to hear disappointing news. Charles' pilot friend refuses to fly Mabel to New York. He gives no reason other than saying, "That bitch does not deserve to be the first woman to fly across The Atlantic."

That comment brings Mabel to tears. The disappointment, however, will not deter her from her goal. "I will find another way," she confidently exclaims. She gets on a boat bound for New York.

Charles can't get away from Mable. In June 1928, they are both in New York. Although their love affair is over, Mabel keeps hounding Charles to fly her across The Atlantic, this time West to East, from North America to England. "Mabel, why don't you just give it up? It is not worth the trouble."

"Maybe not for you, but it is still my dream." She proceeds to hitch a ride on *The Columbia* to Newfoundland, flown by still another pilot. Publicity again abounds about *The Queen of Diamonds'* latest attempt to be the first woman to fly transatlantic to London.

In secret, from the same city, another team is attempting to do the same journey. *The Friendship* will be piloted by William Struts. His passenger will be a demure woman with impressive aviation credentials.

The Friendship takes off on June 17. *The Columbia,* grounded by engine trouble, cannot. The next day, *The Friendship* arrives successfully in London.

Crowds come out in full force to cheer Struts and his passenger for their record-breaking achievement. The woman passenger is the first to greet the crowd from her seat on the plane.

"Thank you all for your kind congratulations. This feat was a long time coming, and I am proud to represent the women of the world here today." She steps down out of the plane to even more applause. Amelia Earhart takes a well-deserving bow.

Mabel Boll is broken-hearted. Her dream is destroyed. Her aviation obsession is over.

****

"Grandpa, Mabel sounds like quite a character."

"She certainly was, Alaine, but she was a whole lot of fun," he adds with a big smile on his face.

"Your life is so interesting. What next happens in your life?"

"Quite a bit. Unfortunately, some of my tales are not pleasant. You might see me in an unfavorable light."

Alaine plants a kiss on Charles' forehead. She has grown fond of the old man. "Grandpa, no matter what comes next, I will always love you."

Charles' face turns bright red; he is humbled by her feelings.

Who is Charles Levine?

PART III: THE CRIMINAL

CHAPTER 1

November 1928---March 1929

Charles and Grace have been separated for seventeen months. He dearly misses his children. Ardith is now four years old. His first child, Eloise, is almost eight. It is time to go home.

Charles drives up to his house in Boston. Eloise is the first to greet him at their front door, followed closely by Ardith. "Daddy's here," Eloise yells out.

He gives both of them a big hug. "How are my girls? You have both grown so."

"We have missed you so much. Are you going to stay here with us now?" Eloise pleads.

"I hope to. You both know how much I love you. Now I must talk to your mother. Where is she?"

Grace walks to the entrance foyer. "Hello Charles, so nice to see you," she says sarcastically. "Why are you here?"

Charles attempts to hug her, but she pulls away. "My flying days are over. I want to be a family again."

"Are your cheating days over also?"

"Yes, that too, I am a changed man. If you take me back, I promise to be a loyal husband. Please believe me. I love you, and I know we can be happy again."

"Our children need a father, and unfortunately that is you. I will forgive you for your past sins, but not any future ones. Welcome home." She kisses him gently on his lips, a smile on her face, caution on her mind.

For the next four months, Charles, Grace, and the children live a contented and peaceful life together. Charles lives up to his promise and is once again a doting husband and father. But Charles, as is his wont, grows impatient. He needs to make some changes.

Under the leadership of its General Manager, during Charles' absence, Brass Balls continues to thrive. Two more plants have been opened, and sales have increased threefold. The stock price rises considerably making Charles' share, as its largest stockholder, worth many more millions. But, despite the accumulated wealth,

Charles is not content---there is no longer an active role for him.

"Grace, I'm thinking about selling my stock in Brass Balls Inc. The time is right."

Grace is unsure. "Sell out, I don't know. What will you do then?"

"The stock market is going wild. I will take all my cash and invest in it. If things go right, I could rival Rockefeller, Vanderbilt, and other barons in wealth. We can move to New York, build a mansion on 5th Avenue, a summer house in Newport, and travel the world. We will be the envy of our faith."

"And if things don't go right?"

"You worry way too much. What can go wrong?"

CHAPTER 2

October 1929---February 1930

The Roaring Twenties are over. The decade of good times, excess wealth, and wild speculation end when the worst stock market crash in the history of the country occurs on October 29, 1929. On this day hundreds of thousands of people lose fortunes and see their net worth shrink to nothing. Panic ensues as these investors are wiped out.

Charles Levine is one of these investors. Charles follows through on his plan to sell his stock in Brass Balls, and from May to October invests the proceeds in speculative stocks. In his dream of becoming one of the wealthiest men in the country, he leverages his purchases through margin accounts and even takes out a large mortgage on his house.

Charles comes home (at least it will continue to be his home until the bank forecloses) that night in shock and in tears. "Grace, I have lost almost everything. All that I have worked for all these years is gone."

Grace, not quite understanding the magnitude of their misfortune responds, "Oh Charles, you are exaggerating. We will recover."

In the following months, Grace realizes Charles did not exaggerate—they will not recover. On the day that the bank puts padlocks on their doors and evicts the family onto the street, she turns to Charles and bitterly says, "You had to invest everything? What could go wrong, you said? I guess we know the answer to that question now. Goodbye Charles, I am leaving you and this time it is for good."

Grace and the children move to New York to live with her brother. Charles stays in Boston, living in a friend's garage. His life will never be the same.

Charles' financial position is worse than being broke. He also is in debt and has legal troubles. He owes the government over $700,000 in back taxes and another $300,000 in Workmen's Compensation claims. They are unrelenting in their efforts to collect.

In addition, Charles' last remaining asset, Columbia Aircraft Corp. faces its own problems. It builds a large aircraft called the *Uncle Sam;* a plane supposedly capable of a range that can circle the globe. It fails miserably. After only twelve flights it is destroyed in a suspicious fire. Charles is hopeful of recovering some funds in the insurance claim but is denied due to his suspected role in arson. The company files for bankruptcy.

In desperation, Charles turns to his old friend, Mabel Boll, for help. They renew their love affair, but she is unable to lend him any money. "Darling, I wish I could help you, but I am nearly broke also," she tearfully claims. Her life has changed for the worse also. She is no longer the *Queen of Diamonds* when her wealthy husband finds out about her numerous affairs and divorces her. On Broadway, her star power fades to just a glimmer after newspapers detail her scandalous lifestyle.

"I have an idea how we can make some money," she says as they lie in bed in her New York apartment. "A former lover of mine in Paris owes me some favors. He can supply us with counterfeit francs."

"Is that the best you can do?" Charles answers. "You want us to become criminals? I do not feel comfortable with that."

"You have any better ideas?"

Charles still has his moral compass, but he is in a desperate state. He thinks over his situation, "*A life of*

74

crime was never before in his thoughts, but if he is to recover, what choice does he have?"

"No," he admits. "When do we leave for France?"

By promising to do a one-woman show aboard the ship, they are able to book passage on an Ocean Liner at no cost to them.

In Paris, they meet Mable's friend at his office. "Hello Mr. Levine, my name is Pierre. Actually, that is not my real name, but you can call me by that alias."

"Hello Pierre, please call me Charles. I understand you are quite good at your job." Pierre shows them a sample of his counterfeit coins. To their naked eyes, they look identical to the real thing.

"My new friend, it is a difficult art. I have been doing it for over twenty years with much success, albeit with much trepidation. But now, let's get down to business."

Mable speaks up, "We are both in dire need of funds. We need all the francs you can spare."

"Mable, my love, for you I will give you all that I have. My compensation will be your past favors and hopefully some future ones."

Mable gives Pierre a long hard kiss. "You are so sweet. I look forward to renewing our friendship sometime very soon."

"I am giving you 500,000 francs, about 100,000 in U.S. dollars, but I must caution you on how to use them. Do not try until you get back to your country. The French merchants and police are much more adept at identifying fakes. When you get back to The States, try to cash them in for dollars in small amounts. You will not arouse as much suspicion that way. Do you understand?"

Mable and Charles nod their heads as Pierre hands them the fake francs. "Thank you," they both say.

"Good luck my friends. Please be careful," Pierre says as Mable and Charles leave his office.

It does not take long for their life of crime to come to a screeching halt, however. They are immediately arrested upon arriving at the New York City port. They do not listen to Pierre's warnings and foolishly pay for their return trip with the fake currency. It does not fool the ship's French quartermaster.

Upon being handcuffed at the port, Charles laments to the arresting officer, "It would appear I used my counterfeit coins foolishly."

****

"Alaine, telling this part of my story is difficult for me. It shows what greed can do to a man; I invested foolishly and destroyed my family in the process. I was trying to find a way to continue to support my family and, stupidly, I turned to crime. It was a big mistake. The moral I hope I have passed on to you today is that crime does not pay. I am so ashamed of my actions."

"Grandpa do not be so hard on yourself," Alaine says. Showing an insight beyond her years, she adds, "We all make mistakes. It is how well we recover from them that is important."

Charles smiles. "Even today those words are comforting. As you will see, I tried my best from that point on to always do what was right and legal."

CHAPTER 3

June 1930---December 1931

Charles suffers a hat trick for his crimes. He is found guilty of violating the Workmen's Compensation Law, making a fraudulent insurance claim, and counterfeiting. He is given a two-year prison term in federal jail and a ten-year probation. How the mighty have fallen!

Prison is difficult for anyone, but especially for a person who has experienced the high life as Charles has done. His jail cell is only ten feet by six feet, the food is awful, and most of the other prisoners are dangerous. But surprisingly, Charles survives unscathed and serves his time as a model prisoner.

Near the end of his sentence, Charles meets a fellow inmate, a German immigrant. The man's legitimate profession is as a carpenter; his criminal vocation is burglary. The man's name is Bruno Richard Hauptmann.

"I understand you despise Charles Lindbergh and require money. Is that correct?" Hauptmann asks Charles as they walk in the yard.

Charles responds quickly, "It is none of your business, but yes, I have had issues with Mr. Lindbergh in the past. As to my financial needs, I am not in this fucking joint because I am flush with cash. I have had some setbacks."

"I have an idea that might solve those issues", says Hauptmann.

Charles comprehends where this discussion is going but is curious to learn what he has in mind. "Keep talking, I'm listening."

"I'm due to get out of here in a month, and I understand your release will be two months later. I need a partner to help me succeed in my plans. Are you interested?"

Charles is not, but he continues to ask questions. "I take it your plan involves some criminal behavior."

"Do you have another way to make some quick money?"

"No, go on."

"Lindbergh and his wife are building a home in New Jersey."

"So, you plan to burglarize their home?"

"No, that is chicken-shit money. This plan is much more rewarding than that. I recently got a call from an inside member of the household. He/she (I do not wish to reveal this person's gender) asks me if I would be willing to participate in a scheme to kidnap and kill Lindbergh's baby boy. There would be $50,000 in it for me."

Levine is appalled at the suggestion of the crime but continues to feign some interest. "What would be my role?"

"I need someone to help me find a way to launder the money. What do you think?"

"I think you're crazy. Sure, I hate Lindbergh, but the loss of a child is serious shit. No parent should suffer that kind of heartbreak, not even Lindbergh. In addition, you will do serious time, if not the electric chair, if you get caught. No, count me out. I want no part of this stupidity."

"OK, there is no harm in asking. I thought your hatred of Lindbergh was sufficient to pique your interest."

"It is not, and I wish you no luck in this crazy idea." Charles walks away shaking his head in disgust.

PART IV: THE WORKING MAN

CHAPTER 1

April---October 1932

After his release from prison, Charles hits rock bottom. He is an ex-con, penniless, and without a home. He moves to The Bronx in New York and is living in a homeless shelter. In his world without much to enjoy, his one saving grace is his love of baseball. But he is no longer a fan of the Boston Red Sox; his new favorite team is now the New York Yankees, where his friend, Babe Ruth, is the star attraction.

The Babe has become the best baseball player of his era and in many experts' opinion the best player ever. After his trade from the Red Sox to the Yankees, he leads his new team to four World Series championships with his astounding home run power. In their latest World Series win against the Chicago Cubs his *called shot* into the centerfield bleachers is considered an amazing historic event.

After the final game of the series, *The Babe* and the Yankees return to Yankee Stadium for a victory celebration—Charles rushes to attend. *The Babe* is arduously signing autographs as Charles approaches him. Despite his ragged appearance, *The Babe* instantly recognizes him. He takes Charles aside, away from the massive crowds. "My friend, I have followed your career from afar. I am so pleased by your accomplishments and disappointed by your current state. How can I help?"

"Babe, I want nothing from you. Your words of wisdom got me started on my successful career. Only my stupidity caused my failures."

The Babe is well known for his generosity. He takes $200 from his wallet and stuffs it into Charles' pocket. "Take this and shut up—I want to help. I am calling our owner tomorrow and getting you a job with the team. He cannot refuse me."

Charles holds back his tears. Once again, this huge and talented man is coming to his rescue. "Babe, you are still the greatest. Thank you so much."

The next week Charles starts work in the Yankee ticket office. It is a low-paying job, but he is grateful for the opportunity. He buys a suit with a portion of the funds given to him by *The Babe and* shows up on his first day clean and optimistic. He is greeted by his superior, a beautiful, twenty-four-year-old woman. High cheekbones, piercing brown eyes, and expertly, coifed black hair emphasize her appearance.

"Hello Mr. Levine, my name is Alana Weinberg. I was told you would be starting today. Welcome to the New York Yankees," she says with a big smile. Her beauty is complimented by a sweet engaging personality.

Just being a small part of the greatest team in sports sends a chill throughout his body. "It's nice to meet you Alana, I look forward to working with you."

"Ok, let's get started—grab a phone and just start taking orders for future games. This is our slow time; games don't start until April. Just you and I will be here until January."

Being alone with a beautiful woman for eight hours a day for three months is a fringe benefit that Charles is quick to adjust to. In the coming weeks, Charles and Alana become good friends.

At first, their relationship consists of only friendly workplace chit-chat, but it quickly grows into more heartfelt conversations.

"I have had an interesting life," Charles says, clearly understating his adventures. "I grew a small start-up company into a leader in its field. I took up aviation as a hobby and set world records. I lost everything in the stock market crash. I became a criminal to try to survive and paid for my mistakes by spending two years in prison."

"Oh my," Alana interjects.

"I regret my decisions. I am trying to turn my life around. Oh also, I have a wife, and I have two children, who love me."

"Wow, that is a lot to experience in a relatively short time. My life is a lot more boring."

"Please tell me about it, but do not belittle your accomplishments. You are a woman who is the head of this department. That is an outstanding achievement for someone so young."

"Thank you, I have worked hard and traveled far to be where I am today. I was born in Berlin, Germany, and immigrated to the United States to attend New York University. My parents and younger brother still live in Germany.

After graduation three years ago, I became a U.S. citizen and I started to work with The Yankees, first as an unpaid intern, then rising through the ranks to my present position."

"I give you a lot of credit. Leaving your homeland and your family could not have been easy."

"No, it was not, but I am glad I did it. It is a difficult time for a Jew living in Germany. I just hope my parents and brother are ok." Alana starts to tear up. She quickly changes the subject, "Tell me about your wife and kids."

"Sadly, my marriage is broken. My wife, Grace, left me when I went broke. I have not seen or heard from her or my children in three years. Our divorce eventually will be final."

Alana takes Charles' hand in hers. "That is a shame. I hate to see marriages end badly." Her smile betrays her comment.

The two agree to have dinner Saturday night at the local Horn & Hardart, an automat, popular during the depression for its low-cost meals. Their conversation turns more personal.

"Alana, what do you do in your spare time?" Charles asks.

"I have been involved in Jewish causes. Antisemitism is growing around the world at an alarming rate."

"It seems we have a lot in common. I am very concerned about that trend too. This guy, Adolph Hitler has some dangerous ideas. His Nazi party must be stopped."

After another hour of talk about Hitler and his growing support in Germany, Alana and Charles head for Alana's apartment on The Grand Concourse, a short walk from Yankee Stadium. Alana breaks out a 15-year-old bottle of Scotch. Prohibition is shortly due to end. The couple celebrates that fact by becoming exceedingly inebriated. Alana moves closer to Charles and kisses him deeply. In her drunken state, she is clearly making advances.

Charles, ever the gentleman, backs up. "I have had a lovely evening—let's not ruin it with something we might both regret tomorrow."

Disappointed, Alana says, "You are too kind. I will see you on Monday."

****

"Alana is my grandmother. Is she not?" asks Alaine.

"You are getting ahead of the story. Be patient, I will eventually get to the family history."

CHAPTER 2

November 1932

Everyone is talking, but not about The World Series, the end of Prohibition, or the Presidential election. They are talking about the so-called *Crime of the Century*. On March 1, the 20-month-old son of Charles and Anne Lindbergh is kidnapped from their home in New Jersey. A ransom of $70,000 is demanded by the kidnapper.

The New Jersey State Police and the FBI immediately start a nationwide manhunt for the culprit, but to no avail. Tragically, the body of the baby is found dead in May. Eight months into the search, the killer is still at large. Although hundreds of tips are sent to the authorities, none pan out. A $25,000 reward is offered without any credible success.

In their office, Alana and Charles discuss the latest news regarding the kidnapping and murder of the child. "It is so sad. Lindbergh is a great hero. To suffer such a loss is heartbreaking," says Alana.

"First of all, Lindbergh is not a hero. Someday I will explain my feelings about him. But you are right about the heartbreak. It is exactly what I told the kidnapper."

"You told the kidnapper? You must explain that statement."

"In prison, I met this guy who said he was going to do it with an accomplice, and he wanted me to be part of his plan. I told him he was crazy. I did not believe he would do it. I now know I was wrong."

"That is some story. Did you tell the authorities the name of the man?"

"I am not a snitch, but this crime was so horrific that I felt compelled to do something. So, I tried. I called the State Police two days after the kidnapping.   They did not show much interest. They said they were getting hundreds of tips and they did not have the manpower to check out every one of them. They did not even want to hear his name. The police and I are not on the best of terms."

"You must try again.   This time call the FBI, anonymously. Now that this is a murder case, they must pay attention to you."

"Ok, I will try again." Charles picks up the phone and dials the hotline set up for the case by the FBI.

The call is picked up on the first ring. "Hello, this is Special Agent Tamis. Please give me your name."

"I would rather not, but I do have firsthand knowledge regarding the Lindbergh kidnapping."

"You and everyone else. We are getting thousands of calls. We give priority to those whose names are provided. In addition, there is a $25,000 reward if your tip results in an arrest and conviction."

"I have my reasons to be anonymous. As much as I would like the reward, I will pass on it."

"If you insist. What is your information?"

"This guy with a German accent told me about a year ago that he was going to commit this crime. His name is Bruno Richard Hauptmann. That's H-A-U-P-T-M-A-N-N. And he said he had an accomplice who is a member of the household who instituted the plan. I do not know the name of the accomplice."

"Do you know the current whereabouts of Mr. Hauptmann?"

Charles is frustrated by the Special Agent's indifferent attitude. "No, I have given you his name—it's your job to find him and the other person involved."

With a total lack of emotion, The Special Agent says, "Thank you for your help. We will investigate in due time. Goodbye."

Charles slams the receiver down. "That was a waste of time."

"Give it time. I read that the FBI follows up on every lead eventually," says Alana.

"I am not so confident."

CHAPTER 3

February---March 1933

The relationship between Alana and Charles evolves. After their first date at Horn & Hardart, they see each other often both at work and after hours. Alana continues to be the aggressor trying to move forward at a rapid pace.

After their fourth date, this time after seeing a romantic movie starring Jean Harlow, Alana passionately kisses Charles in the cab ride back to her apartment. "Charles, I think it is about time we got more physical in our relationship. I can't wait any longer." She playfully tries to unzip his pants.

"Alana, please wait at least until we get upstairs," he nervously implores her. In the apartment, they rip each other's clothes off in record time. Their lovemaking, however, lasts many hours.

"I don't know why we waited so long. I think we are pretty good together," Alana says after taking a long drag on her cigarette.

Charles is quick to agree. "Yeah," he mutters. They both fall into a deep sleep.

The next morning, Alana starts a serious conversation. "We must discuss our future. I refuse to live in sin. I love you and I want to be married."

Charles is hesitant to commit for three reasons. He is still married to Grace with two wonderful children. His finances are such as not to be able to support a new family. And his criminal record is cause for concern. "I love you too, but let's not rush into things. I will move in with you, but before we can get married, I need a divorce first."

Alana is determined. "Make it happen." She then adds "Please".

Grace is living in Manhattan. She has found a job at Macy's selling makeup. Her children, now aged 12 and 9, are well taken care of with the assistance of her brother. She wants nothing to do with Charles.

Charles calls Grace, "Hello darling."

"Don't call me darling," she yells into the phone's receiver. "You ruined my life and the lives of our children. You are a common criminal who has brought shame to our entire family."

"Are you done belittling me?"

"Give me time, I'm sure I can come up with a few more insults."

"I want a divorce, he says."

"Good, I want one too. Here are my terms. I want nothing from you except to never see you again and for you to never see our children until they are over twenty-one."

Charles is silent for a moment. Giving up his children is not what he had in mind. "That is not fair. I love my children and they love me."

"Not fair? Was it fair for you to risk everything for your ego-driven dream of ultimate riches? Was it fair not to be able to put food in your children's mouths? Was it fair to go to prison and leave us to clean up your mess? I'll tell you what is fair. I want you out of my life forever. You have heard my terms. I will not change my position." She slams down the phone.

Charles is stunned. He is heartbroken to be forced to abandon his children but he cannot refute Grace's words.

One month later, Charles appears in the Bronx Courthouse. "Mr. Levine are you in agreement with the terms of this divorce decree?" the judge asks. "By the terms of this agreement, you are never to be in contact with your former wife or your children while they are minors. You do understand?"

"Yes, your honor," he says tearfully.

"Then by the power granted to me by the State of New York, I hereby grant the motion of the plaintiff and dissolve your marriage to Mrs. Grace Levine. So ruled."

Charles leaves the courtroom, head bowed.

Alana will not wait another day. Upon leaving the courtroom, she throws her arms around Charles and yells out, "Thank God that is over. Tomorrow, we get married!"

Charles cannot disagree. "Baby, if that is what you want—that is what we'll do. Make the arrangements."

The next day, March 6, 1933, in the same courthouse as the divorce proceeding, Alana and Charles Levine become husband and wife. Babe Ruth is the only guest.

CHAPTER 4

March 1933---August 1934

At the beginning of 1930, the Nazi Party was a fringe group of malcontents. Most Germans paid little to no attention to its members and its platform. They were considered extremists whose ideology as presented in Hitler's book, *Mein Kampf,* was antisemitism, Aryan superiority, and a totalitarian state. Most found these ideas abhorrent.

By 1933 the impact of Adolf Hitler and his Nazi party in Germany has grown. They are now the most powerful force in the political system. The advance is much too fast and much too terrifying.

In the early months of 1933, Hitler becomes Chancellor, and on Election Day of March 6 (the same day as the wedding of Alana and Charles) The Nazi Party wins the largest number of seats in the German Parliament.

How did this happen? What occurs in this short three-year period that so drastically changes the political landscape?

The Versailles Treaty ending World War I put most of the blame for The War on Germany. Because of its odious terms, the German economy suffers greatly. However, the population perseveres until the stock market crash in the United States at the end of 1929. Its impact on Germany is severe as its economy almost completely collapses. Unemployment, the failure of most banks, and rampant inflation cause a deep depression. Panic ensues.

Hitler seizes on the opportunity. In emotional and charismatic speeches, he promises to void The Versailles Treaty, create jobs, and restore the economy. People start to listen and support him.

Words alone, however, are not enough to effectuate such drastic changes. It is Hitler's use of appalling intimidation and violence that are the main components of his inevitable rise to power.

In quick order, using military-style violence, The Nazi Party pushes through legislation that suspends basic rights and allows Hitler to enact laws without the consent of Parliament. Any opponents of the legislation are arrested and jailed. Hitler's government is now considered a dictatorship.

The rest is easy. All other political parties are banned. All trade unions are closed. Most former political and military leaders are murdered. And, all elections are rigged, so that only Nazis can win. In August 1934 the last remaining voice of reason, President Hindenburg dies.

Hitler now becomes head of state and commander-in-chief of the armed forces as well as head of government. His new title is Fuhrer. He has accomplished his first goal—Germany is now a Totalitarian State.

The worst is yet to come.

****

"That is an interesting history lesson, but what does it have to do with you?" Alaine asks.

"I am laying the groundwork for you to understand what the world was like at this time. My involvement in these matters will be revealed in due time.

CHAPTER 5

September 1934

The lives of Alana and Charles Levine have become quite comfortable. Their marriage has been everything they could have hoped for—loving and stable. Alana has been promoted to executive secretary to the general manager, and Charles is now a top assistant in the ticket office. Their salary increases afford them the ability to buy a small home in White Plains, N.Y.

On September 19 they are spending a leisurely evening at home listening to comedian Eddie Cantor on the radio.

An announcer's voice suddenly comes on. "Good evening, Mr. & Mrs. America and all the ships at sea. We interrupt your scheduled programming to bring you this special report," Walter Winchell, the premier radio newsman of the day, says with his customary flamboyant style.

"In New York today, a suspect in the kidnapping and murder of Charles Lindbergh Jr., the infant son of Charles Lindbergh has been apprehended. The manhunt of over thirty-one months for this culprit is over. We now take you to Washington D.C., where J. Edgar Hoover, the director of the FBI is making a statement for the press."

"Through extensive police work, we are pleased tonight to announce the arrest of Bruno Richard Hauptmann. We are confident that Mr. Hauptmann is the man who committed the horrendous acts of kidnapping and murder of Charles Lindbergh Jr. in March of 1932. Be assured we will prosecute this man to the full extent of the law and be successful in winning a conviction with the appropriate penalties."

Hoover's announcement continues, "We will issue a full statement with more details in the coming days, but as of now, we want to relay two crucial elements that led to this arrest. First, our appreciation goes out to a garage attendant who alertly noticed a ten-dollar bill that was marked as coming from the ransom money. He copied the license plate number of the person who cashed in the bill, which led to the identification of Mr. Hauptmann. We will give the media the name of the attendant at a later date."

"We now also want to inform you of the individual who was the first person to identify Mr. Hauptmann as a possible suspect. In an anonymous call from The Bronx in September of 1932, this man told The Bureau that Hauptmann was highly likely to be the person we were looking for. For his own reasons, the caller did not want to leave his name, but I want to be clear, he was the first person to put us on the trail of Hauptmann. We graciously thank him for his huge assistance. That will be all for tonight, please, no questions. Thank you."

"Wow, that is some report. You should be very proud that you were the one who made that call. You did such a good deed!" Alana walks over to Charles and plants a big kiss atop Charles' head.

"I question what took so long and why there is no mention of the member of the household who was also involved?"

"Who do you think that person was?"

"I have an idea, but it is too crazy to even mention."

****

"Wow," says Alaine. "I must run downstairs and tell Mom and Dad about this."

Alaine finds her mother and father in the living room watching TV. "Did you know that Grandpa helped the police catch the kidnapper of Charles Lindbergh's baby?"

Philip is aghast. "Did he tell you that? That is foolishness. I must talk to him."

He runs upstairs. "What lies are you telling my daughter? Did you tell her you helped capture Bruno Hauptmann?"

"How do you know I did not? The call into the FBI was anonymous." Charles answers proudly.

"I find it very hard to believe."

"Let's just leave it at this—it could well have been me."

Philip is frustrated with Charles' responses. "Your tales are getting more fanciful. When talking to Alaine please keep them to the facts."

"That is exactly what I am doing."

CHAPTER 6

March 1937

Hitler's evil ways continue. His antisemitic views have culminated in a goal to annihilate the whole Jewish race. To start on this insane path, laws have been passed in Germany that strictly define what Jews can and cannot do. Any deviation from allowed conduct is dealt with severe penalties including death. Concentration death camps have been opened in Dachau and Buchenwald.

Fredrick Weinberg, Alana's father, has practiced law in Berlin for over forty years. He is a trusted leader and advisor for the Jewish community during that time. His wife, Fran, is always at his side as his receptionist and secretary.

One of the laws enacted by the German legislature is that all Jewish lawyers must discontinue their practice. Mr. Weinberg has resisted complying with this new law.

On a frigid day near the end of January. Lieutenant Franz Schmitt with two deputies of the Berlin Police Force barge past Fran and rush into Fredrick's office.

"Lieutenant, can't you see I am with a client? Your intrusion is inexcusable---get out of here." Fredrick demands.

Franz Schmitt has recently been appointed by Nazi command to enforce the recent restrictive laws. "You Jew dog, do not tell me where I should be. You have been warned many times to stop your practice of law, yet you continue to do so. You are now under arrest."

One of the deputies approaches Fredrick and attempts to put handcuffs on his wrists. Fredrick, a strong and prideful man pushes him away.

"Do not resist. This can get ugly," warns Schmitt.

Fredrick menacingly approaches Schmitt. "Leave me alone, you Nazi pig."

Schmitt does not take kindly to the insult. He removes his revolver and, without any hesitation, shoots Fredrick squarely in the forehead. Fredrick falls back, blood spurting, instantly dead.

Upon hearing the shot, Fran rushes into the office. "Oh my God," she cries out. She bends down to hold her dead husband. With tears flowing, she screams, "What have you done?" Fran raises her fists and starts banging on Schmitt's chest.

Schmitt once again raises his gun. "You Jew whore, you can join him in hell." He fires, point blank, and hits his target, once again in the forehead. Fran dies.

Peter Miller, Fredrick's client, witness to the entire scene, falls back against the wall, speechless.

Unconcerned with his victims' condition, Schmitt points his gun directly at Miller and yells out, "Tell your Jewish friends what you saw today. We will not tolerate any insubordination."

Schmitt instructs his deputies, "Take these bodies out into the street for all to see what happens when you defy our laws. Jews will learn that we will rid our world of their filth."

Charles comes home late from work to find Alana on the kitchen floor crying hysterically with a telegram in her lap. "They killed my parents. They killed my Mother and Father," she yells out in between her sobs.

Charles bends down to console his wife. "What are you talking about?"

Alana hands Charles the telegram. "Here, read this. It is from my brother, Hans, describing the brutal murder of my parents by the Nazis."

"Darling, I am so sorry," he says as he puts his arms around her. "Those bastards are just evil. They must be stopped. All Jews are in danger."

"My brother is my last surviving relative. He was lucky he was not at my father's office at the time. We must do something to help him evade a similar fate. How do we get him out of Germany and into America?"

"It will not be easy. The latest immigration laws are very restrictive."

"We must try," Alana pleads.

Charles mulls it over in his mind. "I have an idea."

CHAPTER 7

April 1937

The depression in the United States lingers on into the Presidency of Franklin Roosevelt. He is elected in 1932 and re-elected in 1936 with the promise of recovery. His ambitious programs, which he calls *The New Deal,* give hope that the problems of the U.S. economy can be fixed, but it is a slow go.

By 1935, 25% of workers are still unemployed and the atmosphere in the country is still gloomy. Although a segment of the public is aware of the rise of Hitler and his radical views, few show any interest. They are more concerned with their own problems. Most Americans, including political leaders, feel that we should not get involved in any European conflict while we have so many people at home suffering.

It is with this mindset that strict quota laws are enacted. Americans do not want new immigrants competing with current citizens for job openings. In addition, a prevailing fear is that insolvent immigrants will add significantly to the already rising number of public charges.

The quota for visa entry into America from Germany is only about 26,000 per year. With the rampant persecution of Jews and others, starting after the election of Hitler as chancellor in 1933, these visas are in great demand. The waiting list by 1937 is in the hundreds of thousands. To make it even more difficult, the paperwork needed to obtain these visas is extensive. Passports, police certificates, exit permissions, and financial affidavits are required. The chances of a new applicant getting a valid visa are essentially zero.

It is not only the United States that is so restrictive, but almost all countries have similar strict visa policies. Hans Weinberg and thousands of other Jews are essentially stuck in Germany.

"I have inquired about visas out of Germany," Charles tells Alana. "Unfortunately, at this time, it is virtually impossible for us to obtain a legal visa for Hans."

Alana, again, starts to cry. "At this time? At this time? What are you talking about? Within a year, Hans will be in jail or dead. We must get him out now!"

"As I said, I have an idea. It will most likely not be legal and could get Hans and myself in trouble."

"Go for it. What choice do we have?"

"None. I am going to call an old friend and ask for a very big favor."

PART V: THE SECRET AGENT

CHAPTER 1

May 1937

Amelia Earhart and Eleanor Roosevelt, the wife of President Franklin Roosevelt are good friends. Some rumors say they are more than friends. Amelia has been to the White House many times for social gatherings and has even given Eleanor flying lessons. One night, dressed in evening gowns, they leave a White House state dinner to take a short flight on Amelia's plane to party in Baltimore.

They often speak of politics and the growing problems in Germany. Eleanor always seems to be on the most righteous side of the social issues of the day, even if they are not the most popular.

"You know my dearest Amelia, I am not always in agreement with my husband. I can't say that in public. I must always be seen to be in lockstep with him. But Franklin can be a little stubborn and short-sighted."

"How so?" asks Amelia.

"For instance, I feel our country must be more concerned with Hitler's persecution of Jews. It is only going to get worse. I'm worried that this madman will carry out his threats of annihilation. He is capable of anything."

"I must agree. My European friends are afraid his rhetoric and power-crazy attitude will lead to another World War."

"It will come sooner than you think. So far, most Americans are not showing any interest in getting involved, but we must be ready to help."

"I have an old friend who wants to help. I received a call from him recently. He would like to meet with you."

"Who are we talking about?"

"His name is Charles Levine. You might remember him. He set the record back in 1927 as the first passenger to fly from New York to Berlin."

"Yes, I do recall. I also remember he had some trouble with the law."

"Yes, he did.   He made a lot of mistakes, but recently he has turned his life around.   The two of you agree on many issues. I think you should hear him out."

"Upon your recommendation, I will meet with him, but it cannot be at the White House. It must be in private. The press and my husband cannot know I am meeting with an ex-con."

"Great, I will make the arrangements."

Amelia calls Charles. "It is all set. You are meeting with the First Lady next month in New York, at the New Yorker Hotel. I will follow up with you with the exact date and time. The room will be in my name."

"I can't thank you enough. This means everything to my wife and me."

"It was the least I could do for an old flying colleague. You might not know this, but at the time of our first meeting, I was thinking of giving up flying and sticking to writing. There were so many barriers for a woman to overcome. Your enthusiasm inspired me to continue."

"All this time, I thought it was you who inspired me. I guess we both needed that push. Thanks again, I'll see you in a month.

****

"I understand Eleanor Roosevelt was a great person, independent of her husband. I am confused though. What did you mean that Amelia and Eleanor were more than friends?" Alaine asks naively.

"The gossip mills, even up until today, love to spread rumors. For someone your age, it is not necessary to know all the details. Let's just say that the rumors deal with personal choices."

CHAPTER 2

June 1937

At the dot of 2 p.m., Charles knocks on the door of the hotel room. "Welcome Charles," greets Amelia. "It's so nice to see you again."

"Thank you, Amelia. It has been a long time." They hug.

Sitting in the rear of the room is Eleanor Roosevelt. Charles walks over to her and extends his hand. "It is such a pleasure to meet you, Mrs. Roosevelt. You and your husband are doing such great things for this country."

"Don't thank me," says the First Lady. "It is Franklin who does all the work."

"That's not what I hear," says Charles.

Amelia interrupts, "Enough chit-chat. Mrs. Roosevelt's time is very limited. I am going to leave you two to talk. I don't think I should be part of your conversation." Amelia exits the room.

"OK, Mr. Levine, what can I do for you?

Charles tells the First Lady about the murders of Fredrick and Fran Weinberg, and the need to extricate Hans from Germany. "Germany is intent on persecuting all Jews. It will only get worse. Our country must relax our quota laws, or we will witness a massacre of the Jewish faith. It will happen not only in Germany but all over Europe."

Eleanor drops her head, clearly concerned. "I sympathize with your situation. I agree, we should be doing something. It would be the humanitarian and right thing. But The President disagrees, and he is the boss. The American people have made it quite clear they do not want to allow more immigrants into our country. His position is that he must follow the will of the people. I am sorry, but there is little I can do to help you."

Charles is crestfallen. He stares into space, trying to think of what he should do now.

Eleanor sees Charles' obvious frustration. "Do not give up hope. I may not be able to help, but I know of someone who might, but this information must never be repeated as coming from me. His name is William Donovan. We call him *Wild Bill*."

"Who is William Donovan?" Charles asks.

"I have said too much already. All I will say is he holds many of the same beliefs as you do and he is a man of action. You should look him up." Mrs. Roosevelt grabs her coat and heads for the door. "Good luck," she says as she leaves the room.

****

Alaine is impressed. "Meeting with The First Lady was quite an achievement. Amelia must have been a very good friend to set that up."

"Yes, she was. Sadly, it was the last time I saw her." Charles says solemnly. "Not two months later, she would attempt to fly around the globe. Shortly into her flight, all radio transmissions ended. She would never be seen or heard from again."

CHAPTER 3

July 1937

Over the next month, Charles does his research on William Donovan.

Wild Bill Donovan was a World War I hero and a Medal of Honor awardee. He got his nickname, *Wild Bill,* because of his endurance and perseverance in the face of danger. As an attorney, he was Assistant Attorney General during Calvin Coolidge's presidency. His politics are the opposite of Franklin Roosevelt's, focusing on domestic concerns and his friendships with Jews and other minorities. He is a charismatic leader with an enthusiastic and enduring personality.

Starting in 1933 he travels the world to try to understand the heads of state and the politics of countries in Europe and Asia. He wants to learn as much as possible to prepare America for what will be coming. His ultimate goal is to establish an intelligence-gathering agency for the United States, similar in scope to England's MI6.

Currently, *Wild Bill* is in Washington D.C. trying to convince Congress of the dangers that lie ahead in

Europe, and the need for an intelligence and spying agency to protect the interests of the United States.

Charles meets Bill in the lobby bar of The Hamilton Hotel. Bill is an imposing, handsome man of 6' 3". A football player in his youth, he still looks as if he could play linebacker for the New York Giants.

As he takes a swig of his second glass of scotch, he greets Charles with a powerful handshake. "I got a call from Amelia. She says a person in high places recommends I speak to you. Since it comes from Amelia, I am assuming it is The First Lady. So, here I am. What can I do for you?"

Charles tells *Wild Bill* his story and his desire to help Jews in Europe.

"This is not the first time I have heard about the horrors coming out of Germany. There are many Jews like your brother-in-law who want to get out. He takes another sip of his drink and says emphatically, "I can help!"

Before Charles has a chance to ask how Bill continues speaking. "I have been formulating a plan to rescue people. I must warn you that my plan is expensive, dangerous, and clearly against the law. Are you willing to take on this responsibility?"

"I am," says Charles, excited and a little apprehensive. "Mr. Donovan, as a Jew, I feel I must try to prevent the atrocities so many of my faith are facing. I want to help my brother-in-law and others in a similar situation. What do I have to do?"

"The key is Denmark. If we can get Jewish refugees there, which will be hard enough, there will be a way to get them to safety and eventually to the United States. I need you to lead this escape plan. I can provide you with the necessary intelligence, but my name must never be spoken. I am too high profile. If word gets out that an influential American, like me is involved, the repercussions both in The States and abroad could be significant. This operation must be done in secret. Do you understand?"

"Yes," says Charles. "When do we start?"

"Right away. The longer we wait, the more Jews will be murdered. Go home and tell your wife you will be away for months. Also, I can provide you with some funds, but you should raise additional funding on your own. We meet in Paris in two months. That is where our operation begins."

CHAPTER 4

September 1937

In 1936, Hitler curtails many of the restrictions and hateful acts against Jews because of the Summer Olympics being held in Berlin that year. He wants to fool the world into believing he is a benevolent leader. Many will fall for this scam.

By the start of 1937, he is back to his most evil ways. The Nuremberg Laws passed in 1935 brazenly justify the harassment and violence. The beginning stages of the so-called solution to the *Jewish problem* are now in full force.

In quick order, Jews lose their citizenship, the right to vote, what professions they can hold, what schools they can attend, and even who they can marry. Their businesses are taken away, and their wealth and income are taxed at exorbitant rates. Influenced by Nazi propaganda, eventually, most of German society turn against any association with Jews. They will be met with scorn and violence if they do.

German Jews are fearful for their survival. They know they cannot continue to live in Germany with the

119

atrocities forced upon them by this hideous Nazi regime. *But what are they to do? Where are they to go?*

Hans Weinberg, still shaken by the murder of his parents and forced to leave the law school he was attending, is desperate to escape. He speaks to his good friend, Josef Rudolph, "I just got a letter from my sister in America. She and her husband are working on a plan to get me out of here, but it might be dangerous. Do you want in?"

Josef answers instantly, "What do you think? The Nazis have taken away my bakery. I have nothing left. Count me in. What do we have to do?"

"We must sit tight and wait. Hopefully, we will get some news soon."

Charles gets a call from Bill Donovan. "So how is it going? Are you ready to meet me in Paris?"

"I am having a little trouble raising the funds we need, but have no fear, I will do it. Give me a few more days and I will let you know when I will be leaving."

"I am confident of your success. I await your call."

CHAPTER 5

October 1937

There are several Jewish organizations fully aware of what is going on in Germany. The newspapers, controlled by the Nazis, are now even openly publishing articles promoting the extermination of all Jews. Some Americans want to help but raising money for the cause is difficult.

Charles pleads his case to The Anti-Nazi League, a group whose name clearly defines its mission. "We must help our fellow Jews escape the horrors they are facing. Their deaths will be their fate if we do not act now. We cannot help all of them, but even if it is only a few, our efforts will be worth it."

Mildred Stone, the director, is sympathetic to Charles' pleas, "It is hard to believe, but many people are still ambivalent about what is happening in Europe. They do not appreciate the seriousness of the matter. But I do, and so do many of my charitable donors including the financier, Bernard Baruch. Your cause is just. We will raise the funds you need."

"On behalf of the Jews stuck in Germany, I thank you. There are millions of Jews in Europe who will need our help. I only wish I could do more."

A week later, Charles receives the funds he requested. He is now ready to begin his mission.

At the Brooklyn port, Alana hugs Charles tightly before his trip. "My sweet love, please be careful. I want you to return safely with my brother, but do not take any unnecessary chances."

Charles responds, "I'm afraid this whole operation will consist of dangerous chances, but we both know it must be done. I promise you I will return with your brother."

"Your confidence betrays the difficulties that lie ahead of you. I love you." She kisses him goodbye.

Charles walks up the stairs leading to the cruise ship bound for the port of Le Harve, France. At the top, he waves to Alana and then raises his hands above his head in a gesture of victory. "I love you," he yells out.

Rocky seas are present for most of his time on board, but the ship arrives at its destination without incident. Charles spends most of his time on board wondering what plans *Wild Bill* has in mind. He is prepared for the worst.

Bill Donovan greets Charles as he exits the ship, "Welcome to France. We have no time to waste. We start right now. Our first stop is to meet with our forger. His name is Jean-Paul."

After a short ride to Paris, Bill and Charles arrive at an old warehouse. After three knocks, a familiar face opens the door. Charles is stunned. "Pierre, it is so nice to see you again."

"My name is now Jean-Paul. As I explained to you last time, I change my aliases often. In my business, you must take this precaution."

Charles explains to Bill his previous association with Pierre/Jean-Paul. "This man was my counterfeiter a few years back. He did a magnificent job with some fake francs. Unfortunately, I did not follow his advice and I was apprehended."

"I thank you for never giving up my name," says Jean-Paul. "Now, I understand you require some forgeries. It will be my pleasure to help you again, but this time I must be paid."

"No problem, my friend." Charles takes a handful of bills out of his satchel and hands $2000 to Jean-Paul. "I can assure you they are real." Charles and Jean-Paul share a laugh.

Bill interrupts the reunion and gets right to the business at hand. "We will need about twenty fake visas and passports for our plans. Are you up to this task?"

"Give me enough time and I will give you forgeries that will fool the best border guards. I have prepared one already as you instructed me to do. I will start the paperwork immediately on others, but I will need pictures of all the people involved."

Bill replies, "We will get the pictures you need, but let's start now with Charles." Charles stands in front of a white background and Jean-Paul snaps the photo. Jean-Paul develops the film and then expertly places the picture on a fake passport.

"My friend, you are now Charles Brown." He hands Charles the fake passport along with a phony tourist visa. "You can now go to Germany without fear," says Jean-Paul confidently.

"I hope you're right," says Charles, not as confident.

"That's one down and 19 to go. We will have a courier return here as soon as possible," says Bill. "Until then goodbye."

Charles and Bill head for a tiny bistro down the street. As they sip on their expressos, Charles asks Bill anxiously, "What is the plan?"

Bill replies, "It's complicated."

****

"Grandpa, I can't wait to hear about the escape plan, but first tell me what Charles Lindberg has been up to all this time."

"Ok, if you insist. I am a little foggy about all the dates, but I will try to remember the best I can. I will tell you that *this hero* was doing all he could to undermine the world's efforts to stop the horrors of Hitler's regime. I say emphatically that this Jew-hater was not a nazi-sympathizer, but, in fact, was a full-fledged NAZI himself."

CHAPTER 6

October 1937

After the trial and execution of Bruno Hauptmann, Charles Lindbergh and his wife, Anne, move to England in 1935. They want to escape all the publicity surrounding the kidnapping and death of their first child.

During his stay in England, Lindbergh travels many times to Germany. His goal is to evaluate and advise on the state of German aviation. He is impressed by what he sees. He finds the technology, power, and size of their air force to be outstanding. His views will eventually influence France to avoid conflict and hinder Britain in its defenses.

The most outrageous indication of Lindberg's pro-Nazi leanings occurs at a dinner he is invited to by Herman Goring, Germany's top air force general. Goring, in full military uniform, praises Lindbergh for his assistance, and then asks him to step forward. Lindbergh does so with a smile.

Goring then announces to the large crowd attending, "On behalf of my Fuhrer, Adolf Hitler, it is my honor to bestow upon Charles Lindbergh, the greatest aviator of our time, The Commanders' Cross of the Order of the German Eagle. It is the highest honor we can grant to a non-German."

Goring places the medal around Lindbergh's neck. Lindbergh's smile gets even bigger. "Thank you, Herr Goring," he says. "I accept this honor with much gratitude."

All Jews, as well as most others from around the world, are shocked. They ask, in wonderment, *"How can this supposedly loyal American accept this prize from such an evil empire?"*

With the winds of war circulating throughout Europe, Lindbergh talks of capitulation. In many speeches, he tells the leaders of England and France, "For your own good, refrain from your claims of violations of the Versailles Treaty and other aggressive actions. Any military action by you will be easily defeated by the superior German forces."

In America, he gives a national radio speech, "We must stay isolated and remain neutral in any European conflict. Germany is a strong, righteous nation that should not be provoked. The truth is that they are good people, doing what they feel is best for their country. I share their belief that eugenics is a valid, much needed, scientific theory."

All intelligent people realize his rantings are thinly veiled rationalizations for the travesties being planned against all Jews. Lindbergh's antisemitism grows even stronger.

****

Charles stops his narrative abruptly. "I cannot continue. Lindbergh's words and actions are so hateful, even today—fifty years later, they make me sick. We will talk again. There is much more to say about Mr. Lindbergh."

"I do have one question," says Alaine. "What is eugenics?"

"It is a horrible theory that Hitler used to justify his actions. It is the belief that with selective breeding only the strongest will survive, and a master race will be created. In his warped mind the extermination of Jews, homosexuals, the handicapped, and other inferior races, will result in a stronger, better human race."

"And Lindbergh agreed with this?"

"Sadly, yes. Goodnight my child."

CHAPTER 7

October 1937

Still at the bistro, on their third cup of expresso, Charles and Bill go over their plan for a second time.

"We are naming this operation *Let's Go,* because of the need for speed and precision," says Bill. "The German police are acutely aware that Jews are desperate to escape, so all your movements must be carefully orchestrated to avoid capture. I am leaving you today— the rest of the operation is in your hands. I am counting on you."

"I am ready to proceed," says Charles. "Let me repeat my first steps. Tomorrow morning, I board the Paris-Berlin train. I show my forged documents to the border officials to gain entry. My cover story is that I am an American tourist who is an art enthusiast, looking forward to seeing the works of German artists in the Berlin Museum. At the first train stop in Germany, I will meet up with Emil Gutmer who will be my translator and courier. He will recognize me by the New York Yankee hat I will be wearing. He will greet me with the code words *Let's go.* I will respond *Let's Go Now."*

Bill interrupts, "I know all the cloak-and-dagger stuff sounds corny, but in my experience, it pays to be ultra-cautious. It is also wise that in any correspondence we use code names. I will be *Wild One,* you will be *The Aviator.* Emil is a good man. His code name will be *The Gut.* He is a German citizen who is loyal to our cause. I have worked with him before. He can be trusted."

"I cannot afford to doubt you—only my life is at stake." Charles wipes his brow nervously. "When we arrive in Berlin, Emil will take me to a safe house, where Hans, my brother-in-law, is staying. I will go over all the arrangements and get him and his friends ready for the next steps in our escape plan."

"Excellent but be prepared for some things not to go as planned—that always happens. You must think quickly and improvise if necessary."

"Do not worry. Through my many travails in life, the need for fast decisions has occurred often."

For the next two hours, Bill and Charles go over all the details numerous more times until Bill is confident that Charles has the operation down pat. "OK, tomorrow you leave—good luck." *Wild Bill* shakes Charles' hand, gets up from the table, and walks silently away into the night.

Charles suffers through a sleepless night. At 6 a.m., he gets out of bed and walks to the Paris train station.

Charles hands his forged papers to the German border official there. He looks suspiciously at them. "We do not have many American tourists going into Germany right now," the guard says in heavily broken English. "What is the reason for your visit, Mr. Brown?"

Charles explains his love of German art.

"Very wise of you. We have many great artists. Who are your favorites?'

Charles freezes—he knows nothing about German art. As Bill had warned, it does not take long for Charles to hit a bump in the road. Charles, trying to think of an appropriate answer, stammers, "I-I-I do not have any favorites. My love of art includes all German masters."

The guard looks at Charles' papers even more thoroughly and then checks his watch. The line of people waiting behind Charles is quite long. Annoyed, the guard says "I would like to check your credentials again, but I do not have the time. You may go."

Charles grabs his papers and rushes onto the train, much relieved.

Three hours into his ride, he looks out the window and views the Rhine River as the train enters Germany.

There is no turning back now. He puts on his Yankee cap as the train makes its first stop one hour later in Luxembourg. Passengers flow in. Bill has given Charles a detailed description of Emil. He does not see him— bump number two is occurring.

Charles sits patiently. It is a big train and Emil is not aware of exactly where Charles is sitting. After forty-five minutes his patience has worn thin. Suddenly, a man approaches him from behind. "Let's go?" the man says. It is more a question than a statement.

Charles responds, "Let's go now?" also in question form. "You are *The Gut*, correct? Where have you been?"

"Yes, I am, and you are *The Aviator*. I could not find you—I was expecting to see a blue cap. Your cap is white."

"I too am surprised. Bill said nothing about a beard and a mustache."

"I have grown this facial hair since I last saw Bill. I guess I should have told him."

Emil sits down next to Charles. "We have a lot to do. We better be more in sync for the rest of our operation," says Charles.

Emil nods. "Yes sir."

Seven hours later, the train approaches Berlin. A conductor passes by and announces the stop. "We arrive in Berlin in ten minutes—have all your identification papers ready."

"I was unaware that they would be checking our papers when we disembark. Is that normal?" Charles asks Emil.

"In the last few months, they have gotten very cautious. Do not worry, it is just a formality."

Charles worries, nonetheless. The more times he must show his phony identification the more likely he will be caught.

Emil proves to be right, the official only gives a passing glance at Mr. Brown's ID as Charles exits the train.

On Berlin soil for the first time since his historic flight ten years ago, Charles is relieved to be in familiar surroundings. With Emil by his side, they grab a taxi and head for the safe house.

"You can drop us here," says Emil after a twenty-minute ride.

On the street, Charles asks, "Which house is ours?"

"It is about three blocks away. You cannot be too careful—I did not want the cab driver to know the exact location."

"Very smart," says Charles.

At the safe house, a solidly built young man opens the door. "Charles?" he asks.

Charles nods. "And you must be Hans?" They hug.

Hans speaks English well. "I am so glad to see you. What you are doing for us is so kind—you are a lifesaver. The damn Nazis are getting worse. There is talk that they will be shipping all Jews to concentration camps shortly. I have seventy people including eight children ready to go with you."

"Seventy people? We were expecting no more than twenty. I don't think we can handle that many."

"We must! We cannot leave anyone out. Death awaits anyone who stays."

Charles thinks hard to himself, "*Donovan warned me about obstacles I might face, but I never expected this.*" He puts his arms around Hans and lovingly says, "We will find a way."

CHAPTER 8

November 1937

Denmark is a small country adjoining the northern border of Germany. The border is only forty miles wide. It lies approximately 400 miles from Berlin. In November Denmark is a magnificent, beautiful country with colorful leaves and a smattering of snow. At present it is free of Nazis.

It is the first step in the plan for Charles, Hans, and other Jewish refugees to escape Germany and find a safe place to live. Although there are relatively few Jews living in Denmark, the citizens there know full well what the Jews in Germany are facing. They are anxious to help. The problem is getting to the border undetected and getting into the country through the border barriers. It was going to be difficult enough to smuggle in twenty people. Smuggling seventy people raises so many more issues.

Charles, Hans, and Emil discuss the situation. "We will need additional counterfeit papers, extra modes of transportation, and more complex strategies," says Charles.

"It must be done. I made promises. I will leave no one behind," pleads Hans.

Emil is worried. "We will need more time, which we don't have."

Charles stops to think. "We will have to break into groups of twenty to thirty people, separated by enough time not to bring suspicion upon us. Emil, you will return to Paris tomorrow with pictures of the first group and return to us when the forgeries are completed. Also, bring enough film so we can take pictures of everyone else. In the interim, Hans and I will figure out further details."

"Jean-Paul will need more money,' says Emil.

Charles takes out $3000 and hands it to Emil. "Tell him there will be more coming to him if he works fast."

The next morning, Emil boards the train for the return passage to Paris. With his German passport, he has no trouble getting past the border officials. Upon his arrival in Paris, he immediately heads to Jean-Paul's warehouse.

"Seventy forgeries?" Jean-Paul exclaims. That will take some time. I can give you the twenty I have already prepared and another ten in two days. The rest will have to wait."

"We will be patient to a point. Here is another $3000 for your troubles."

In Berlin, Hans and Charles are deep in conversation. Charles speaks first, "The original plan was for twenty people to go on a fake skiing vacation to Esbjerg, a town on the east coast of Denmark. We can increase that to thirty without much trouble. We will be taking the train. The remaining two groups of twenty must remain in Berlin for the time being. I owe it to your sister for us to be in that first group. We will also include the children and their parents on that trip. Do you have somebody who can oversee the people remaining?"

Yes, my friend, Josef Rudolph, and his identical twin sisters, Faye and Frida, are capable."

"Good. Let's make the second group, students of architecture. They will go by bus to the border. They will leave a month after us. The third group will be history buffs. They will go in two trucks a month later. Before we leave, we will make the necessary arrangements."

"Sounds good."

"Sounding good is not enough. It must be perfect."

****

Alaine sits on the edge of her seat, thrilled by this adventure. "This story would make a great movie. Is there a happy ending?"

"Sadly, not for everyone."

CHAPTER 9

December 1937

Emil returns with thirty fake passports and visas. At the safe house, Charles inspects all the papers. "Emil, you have done a wonderful job—these all look great. All the names are non-Jewish sounding."

"Don't thank me. Jean-Paul is a masterful artist."

"Don't sell yourself short. You are taking great risks. You know full well what will happen to you if you are caught. We Jews are very appreciative. What motivates you to help us so?"

"As a German, I am embarrassed by what has become of our great country. We used to be proud, caring people. We now have a madman as a leader, and our citizens follow him like ignorant sheep. I am doing my little part to undermine his crazy ideas. I am fearful that it will get much worse, but I will do all I can as long as I am living and breathing."

"I only wish there were more Germans who think the way you do."

"Sadly, there are few. The propaganda machine of *The Reich* is a powerful tool that has brainwashed so many intelligent people. Hopefully, one day smarter, kinder minds will once again lead us. I pray that day comes soon."

"We all do if Jews are to survive."

At that moment, Hans walks into the room with three others. Hans does the introductions, "Charles, this is Josef Rudolph and his twin sisters, Faye and Frida." The sisters are tall statuesque beauties, each with long blond hair. "As I told you, they are good friends who are willing and able to help us with our plans."

"We are so thankful you are here," says Josef. "What can we do to help?"

"First, we must appraise the details of the plan to all who are escaping with us. Where is everyone living?"

Faye answers, "We are all still in our homes, but I don't know how long that can continue. The Nazis are starting to confiscate everything from the wealthier houses. It will not be long before all Jewish homes are affected."

Josef asks, "Are the plans in place to move fast enough?"

Hans answers the questions. "We will go as fast as possible, but we cannot raise suspicion by making foolish mistakes. As of now, all of our people must remain where they are. Meeting as a group would be dangerous. I will pass the word by going to each home."

Charles continues the discussion. "The plan is to escape in three groups over the next two months. Hans and I will lead the first group, leaving at the end of the week. Faye and Frida will lead the second group the following month. Finally, Josef will head the last group a month later. I will go over all the necessary details in the coming days. Is everyone clear so far?"

Everyone nods their heads.

The day before the planned escape, Hans and Charles meet one last time in preparation. "Have you been to all the homes of the people who are leaving with us?" asks Charles.

"Yes, of course. They have their papers with their new names. They will meet us tomorrow at the train station at 8 a.m. They are aware that they supposedly are going on a skiing trip to a resort near Esbjerg. They will have a small suitcase with them and are hiding any cash or valuables they have, in them. They are nervous, yet excited. They are anxious to leave Germany," says Hans.

"How old are the children?"

"They range in age from four to ten. They know to be quiet and stick closely to their parents."

"Good, I hope they don't do anything stupid."

"The adults are asking what happens when they get to Denmark. Where will they be living?"

"The less they know, the better."

PART VI: THE HERO

CHAPTER 1

December 1937

The train ride from Berlin to Esbjerg is a scenic trip of about ten hours, making several stops along the way. All the refugees board the train without incident. But the critical portion of their trip will occur when they encounter the border officials in Flensburg, the last German city before the border to Denmark. Charles and Hans both expect a very thorough examination of their papers there.

Hans is the spokesman for the group. "Everyone stay seated," he tells his people as they arrive in Flensburg. "I will talk to the official first."

"Your papers please." the German official sternly barks at Hans. At this point, the Danes have relinquished all authority for border crossings to German officials.

"Yes sir," replies Hans politely. He hands his visa and passport to the guard. It identifies Hans as Hans Mueller, the alias he is using.

"Mr. Mueller, what is the reason for your trip to Denmark?"

He is ready to respond with rehearsed answers. "The group behind me are members of a skiing club. We are going skiing near Esbjerg."

"You do know there are many great skiing resorts in Germany?"

"Yes, but this club likes variety. We have skied most of the German slopes previously."

"Do you have your train tickets to return to Germany? A round-trip ticket is customary."

Hans is not prepared for this question. He quickly improvises his answer. "We do not know what date we will return so we only bought one-way tickets. We are hopeful the weather will be good enough for a lengthy stay."

The guard, by his expression, is not convinced by Hans' answers. He turns to Charles. "Your passport and visa, sir."

"Mr. Brown, you are an American. You were in Germany as a tourist. Now you are going to Denmark to ski—why is that?"

"I met Hans, and he was kind enough to invite me on this trip. I could not refuse."

The guard moves down a row to speak to a woman with a five-year-old child sitting behind Hans. "Madam, where is all your ski equipment?"

The woman is surprised by the question. She alertly thinks of something. "We shipped it ahead. We thought it would be much easier that way. "

Before the guard moves on, the child yells out. "We are going to live in Denmark."

The mother puts her hand over the child's mouth. "He means we are going to live in Denmark while we are skiing there."

The guard returns to talk to Hans, more suspicious than ever. "Something is not right here. I want all of you to meet with my supervisor. I will get him. He is in the next car."

Hans pulls the guard aside and secretly hands him two hundred German Reichsmarks. "There is no need for that. We are all loyal German citizens looking forward to a fun vacation. We don't want any headaches. Certainly, you can understand that."

The guard softens his attitude. "Yes, I guess I can, but I hope I do not regret this." He puts the bribe in his pocket and quickly stamps everyone's passports. As he leaves, he turns back and yells out, "Have a good trip."

"I did not want to do that, but I had no choice," Hans says to Charles.

"You did the right thing. Let's hope it does not come back to hurt us," says Charles.

Four hours later, the train arrives in Esbjerg. They all yell out in glee, most with tears in their eyes.

****

"It must have been very difficult for these people to abandon their homeland and move to another country?" asks Alaine.

"Yes, it was. Many of them had family in Germany for generations. But difficult times demanded difficult decisions. This one was lifesaving."

CHAPTER 2

January 1938

Emil goes to Paris once again and then returns to Berlin with forged documents for twenty more people.

Josef has gotten word from Charles about the first group's safe arrival in Denmark. He also learns of the troubles they encountered along the way. To be better prepared, precautions are taken to avoid similar issues.

Faye and Frida are ready to lead the next group on a bus to the German/Denmark border and beyond to Esbjerg. They receive last-minute directions from Josef at the safe house. "Faye, are you confident you can drive the bus we acquired?"

"If you recall, I regularly drove the truck for deliveries for our bakery. This bus has the same transmission and controls. To be safe, I have practiced for two days. I will have no problem."

"Good, and you know the route?"

"I will be the navigator," says Frida. "We will stay off all the major highways and stick to the smaller local roads. The border crossing we are going to is the smallest and the most remote, near the western end. Also, everyone knows our cover story—we are architectural enthusiasts who are looking forward to seeing the most interesting buildings in Denmark."

"And the precautions we spoke about, you have them safely packed away?"

"I have them right here in my sack. I will keep them out of sight," answers Frida.

"Great, it seems that you two have everything under control. Everyone will assemble here at 9 a.m. tomorrow. You have a long journey ahead of you. I wish you luck— your lives and the lives of eighteen others depend on it."

Faye gives an optimistic guarantee, "Don't worry, big brother. I promise you we will make it!"

The next morning, twenty brave souls board the bus headed for Denmark. Through the bumpy back roads, ten hours later they arrive at the border crossing. It is the dead of night. There are only two German guards stationed at the crossing. Once again, all border crossings from Germany into Denmark are manned solely by Germans. One official walks slowly towards the bus. "Oh shit," Faye yells out as the official appears clearly in the headlights of the bus.

"What's wrong?" Frida frantically asks.

"The border guard—we know him. His name is Horace Schmitt. He was a student with us in our history class in high school. What are the odds of that?"

Frida is stunned, "It is the most incredible bad luck. What should we do? He knows our real names and that we are Jewish. Our fake papers will do us no good."

The remaining passengers on the bus overhear the conversation of the sisters and are justifiably frightened. They gallantly withhold their screams.

Faye proposes a solution. "Frida, if I remember correctly, Horace was fond of you. Didn't he ask you out on a date?"

"Yes, but I wanted no part of him. I turned him down quite coldly."

"It's time to warm up to him. Maybe you can use your feminine skills to get us out of this."

"I will try!"

Faye opens the door to the bus to let Horace in. He stands in the aisle and surveys the situation. Horace immediately recognizes Faye and Frida. "Well, if it isn't the Rudolph sisters, the prettiest girls in our high school. As if he doesn't know, he smugly asks, "What brings you two and a busload of other Jews here so late at night?" Are you trying to escape the country?"

Frida gets out of her seat and affectionately greets him. "Horace, it has been a long time—it's so nice to see you again. You look so handsome in that uniform."

"Oh, now you like me. It's a little late for that. You had your chance years ago. Now I hold the upper hand. Vengeance will be mine."

"There is no reason to talk like that. Can't we discuss this matter like old friends?" Frida puts her arms around Horace's shoulders attempting to embrace him.

Horace pulls away—he has been indoctrinated well in the ways of the Nazis. "Don't think for a minute that you can pull that shit on me. You are all Jewish scum." He pulls out his gun. He screams at everyone on the bus, "I am arresting you all in the name of the *Third Reich.*" The passengers stay seated and silent, afraid to move.

Frida wisely sees that her charms are not working. She tries another tactic. She pulls out of her bag one of the precautions she brought with her, an envelope full of money. "Horace, you were such a nice boy, you don't need to be so mean. Here are five hundred Reichsmarks for your troubles. Please can you look the other way and let us go tonight."

"Are you kidding me? Now you are trying to bribe me. If I took that, my superiors would kill me instantly. You whore, you are crazy to think I would violate my oath for you and your Jewish friends."

Horace turns his back on Frida and walks down the aisle of the bus. Waiving his gun, he orders the refugees to stand up. "No one will be hurt if you follow my ...." A gunshot rings out. Horace is unable to finish his command. Frida has reached into her bag once again and retrieved her second precaution—her gun. She has hit Horace squarely in his neck with her shot. He screams in agony as blood rushes from the wound.

He turns to face her. "What have you done?" She fires again and hits him right between the eyes. Horace falls dead.

Frida answers Horace's last question. "I killed you before your fellow Nazis could kill us all!" Everyone applauds.

Faye exclaims, "Your sharpshooting skills are impressive."

"Very funny—He was only three feet away—I could not miss. Now get us out of here."

Faye presses down hard on the gas pedal. Right In front of her stands the other guard. "Stop, stop," he yells out. Faye ignores his pleas as the bus picks up speed. The guard moves aside at the last moment—he sees Frida through the window, holding up her gun. He fires his gun repeatedly. The bullets harmlessly ricochet off the bus.

Faye screams, "There is a wooden barrier in front of us. What should I do?"

Frida responds, "Go right through it." Faye does so. The barrier demolishes into splinters. Frida again yells out, "Go faster." The guard continues to fire his weapon with no effect.

Two hundred yards further down the road, the bus is beyond the range of the gunfire, but the passengers can still faintly hear the ineffective demands of the guard, "Stop, stop."

The bus keeps going, passing over the border. "Not today!" Faye answers. She, Frida, and eighteen other Jews have escaped into Denmark.

CHAPTER 3

January 1938

There is no *Jewish Problem* in Denmark. The Danish government and its citizens are very sympathetic to the dangers facing its native Jews as well as the refugees coming from Germany and other European countries.

Although the political leaders are not outwardly supportive of refugees coming into their country because of the strict quota laws, the enforcement of expelling illegal Jewish immigrants is minimal.

In fact, to their credit, many Danes are assisting refugees in many ways including providing clothing, food, and shelter. Their morality and ethics compel them to exhibit these highly humanitarian efforts despite laws to the contrary.

Charles and Hans meet Dr. Karl Baum at his suburban estate just outside Esbjerg a day after arriving in Denmark. Dr. Baum is a noted and respected doctor, who is one of the leaders of the Danish Resistance Movement. That group are the ones who are providing the needed assistance for Charles, Hans, and their charges.

"I hope you have been satisfied with your accommodations so far. Our goal is to keep you hidden and safe during your stay in Denmark. Each of you will have a home," assures Dr. Baum.

"Thank you. All of your people have been so considerate for the last month," replies Charles. "We are grateful. Hopefully, one day we can repay the favor."

"About 8000 Jews are living in Denmark. We acknowledge there is danger ahead for us. My group is committed to resisting the Nazis as best we can. I am sure your experience in defying the Germans will come in handy one day," replies Dr. Baum.

After lunch at Dr. Baum's home, Charles and Hans await the arrival of the bus with Faye, Frida, and the other refugees to join them.

Hours later than the scheduled time, Faye pulls the bus up to the house. Charles and Hans share a sigh of relief.

"Where have you been? We were so worried that something went wrong," says Charles.

Faye answers in an understated calm voice, "You can say that. I took a slow circular route. I was afraid I was being followed."

154

For the next few minutes, Frida describes the problems they faced, and the ultimate deadly solution. She is shaken by the telling of her involvement. Charles and Hans are horrified but understanding.

Hans takes the tearful Frida aside. "Killing someone, especially someone you knew could not have been easy, but it was the only choice you had. You saved twenty people—you are a hero."

"I don't feel like a hero. I feel like a murderer."

"We are in a time of crisis. Do you think Lieutenant Schmitt felt like a murderer when he killed my parents? We must put aside our previous moral beliefs to do what must be done. We might not be in armed combat, but this is war!"

Frida is silent for a moment. She can only whisper, "Thank you." There is an obvious feeling of affection between the two of them as they walk back to Charles and Faye.

"What did you do with the body?" asks Charles.

"We stopped about two miles from the border and dumped it into the woods. Some of the men buried it in the snow. Hopefully, it will not be discovered until the spring," Fay answers.

"Good. I will dispose of the bus somehow. Although we are safe with the Danes, Germans will be looking for you and Frida. They don't take kindly to the killing of one of their own. We must be careful. Did anyone see your faces?"

"I don't know. It was dark and the other guard was a few yards away."

"Let's hope he cannot make an identification. In the meantime, we will get everyone settled into homes. We will sit tight and wait until the final group arrives next month."

"Are we going to stay in Denmark?"

"Yes, for as long as it is safe. We will move on to our final destinations when it is wise to do so."

CHAPTER 4

February 1938

Emil goes to Paris one last time. "We need just twenty more forgeries. Are they ready?" he asks.

Jean-Paul responds, "Give me just a few minutes. I am putting the finishing touches on them. Sit down and have a glass of wine."

"Thank you. I will."

"Good, if you don't mind, I will take a break and join you. Since this is the last time we will be working together, I must tell you how much I admire you for taking these risks to help your Jewish friends. You are a brave man."

"Thank you. I am doing my small part to try to right so many wrongs. I do not understand why more Germans are not resisting the madness of the Nazis to do the same."

"I fear my French countrymen are also turning a blind eye to what is happening. In my opinion, it won't be long before our country will be facing the dangers of German aggression."

"You are right. With Hitler as its leader, anything is possible."

"Tell me, what are your plans going forward?"

"I am going back to my home near Munich. I have a small house on a lake there. I long to relax and fish the hours away. My time as a resistance fighter is over. I fear it is a losing battle."

"I wish you a long and peaceful existence."

"One can only hope."

Jean-Paul finishes his handiwork and hands the forgeries to Emil. "Good luck, my friend." In the customary French tradition, Jean-Paul kisses Emil on both cheeks. They hug goodbye.

On the train back to Berlin, Emil falls asleep. He dreams of better times.

Emil bangs on the door of the safe house. It is safe, no longer. Captain Franz Schmitt opens the door. After murdering the Weinbergs, he is elevated to being an officer in the Schutstaffel (the feared military-style police force, commonly known as *The SS).* He is accompanied by two privates. "Emil Gutmer, you have been a busy boy. Back and forth to Paris so many times." Schmitt pulls out his gun. "Your traveling days are over—you are under arrest," he says.

Emil sees Josef in the rear of the room, handcuffed to a chair. He realizes his dreams of returning home are over. He says nothing.

Schmitt continues his tirade. "Did you think we were going to let you get away with these treasonous acts? We have been following you for months." Schmitt grabs the satchel Emil is holding. All the forged documents fall to the ground. "Just as I suspected, you have been helping the Jews escape. This treachery now comes to an end, and tomorrow morning you will meet your fate."

Schmitt turns to his men, "Take him away and lock him up."

Josef yells out to his friend. "Emil, thank you. We did our best."

"Shut up, you Jew bastard," Schmitt responds. "Your death and that of your friends will come also, slowly and painfully."

There is no trial. The next morning, Emil is strapped to a wooden post in the middle of the largest public square in town. Hundreds of witnesses are forced to attend. Schmitt leads the spectacle. "Today we show you what happens when an enemy of our glorious *Third Reich* disobeys our laws and assists the filth of this nation." He raises his hand, looking directly at the six soldiers pointing their rifles at their intended target. He quickly lowers his hand and yells "FIRE!"

****

Alaine breaks into tears. Charles tries to console her. "I'm so sorry that I had to tell you this part of the story, but you must understand that these were very difficult times. We tried to save as many as we could, but there was so much death—too much to fathom."

Alaine tries to dry her eyes. "What happens to Josef and the other nineteen Jews who were going to escape with him?"

"I am sorry to report, they are all arrested, along with many others. They are packed into trains and shipped to concentration camps. Their fate there is of unimaginable horrors." Charles hesitates and dabs his eyes with a handkerchief. "I will not burden you now with more details—they are so horrific."

Alaine again cries, this time uncontrollably.

CHAPTER 5

February 1938

Charles waits for Josef and his group. They are three days late. His worst fears are realized when he gets a telegram from Bill Donovan.

Aviator: sorry to report—I have bad news. My spies in Berlin report that Emil has been executed and Josef and his group have been caught and are headed to concentration camps. Nothing we could do. Continue to hide and be safe where you are. Future plans will be discussed at a later date. Good luck.

Regards, Wild One

Charles is stunned. He knows that deaths were always a possibility, but it is still deeply hurtful. Even though fifty people currently are free from German rule, he wanted to lead all seventy of them to safety.

He can't help but second guess. He mutters to himself, "*What other precautions should I have taken?*"

Charles gathers both groups at Dr. Baum's house to break the bad news. Everyone is heartbroken. Frida

161

and Fay scream out, "Oh no, my poor brother!" They try their best to console each other.

Hans tries to stay calm, but he can't contain himself, he cries out, "It is such a shame—Emil was a friend and a hero. He will be missed."

They all lower their heads in prayer.

After a day of mourning, Charles again gathers everyone together. "We must now discuss our plans going forward. Although we are currently satisfied with our conditions here in Denmark, we cannot stay indefinitely. The Nazis will be looking for the murderers of their border official. In addition, many military experts predict that Denmark will someday be occupied by German forces. We cannot put the Danes who have been protecting us in further danger. We must be concerned with their welfare as well as the safety of all Jewish Danes."

"Where and when can we go?" asks Faye.

"There are only two places that we should consider—America and Sweden," answers Charles.

"As to when—that is an open question. There are many factors to consider, most of which are out of our control. In the meantime, we sit tight and wait. Before we can even think of leaving, I propose there will be much more for us to do. In my opinion, the Nazis have many more heinous ideas in mind."

CHAPTER 6

November 1938

Charles, unfortunately, is proven right. The Nazis do have other insidious plans. On the nights of November 9 and 10 Kristallnacht (the night of broken glass) takes place.

Kristallnacht is a scourge of violence against all Jews throughout Germany, Austria, and Sudetenland. Hundreds of Jews are killed, and thousands are arrested. The violence includes attacks against synagogues, Jewish businesses and homes. Fires are left to burn, windows are shattered, and people are beaten. The Nazis organize this violence to make clear their intention—no Jew is safe from incarceration or death.

New laws follow that deprive Jews of their property, and their ability to work or go to school. They are basically removed from all means of economic and social life. Antisemitism is in full throttle. The worst consequence is German citizens stay silent---a true indication of their indifference to the atrocities.

Word of these horrific actions filters down to Charles, Hans, and the Rudolph girls in Denmark. They

164

are shocked but not surprised. To them, it is just another validation of their decision to leave Germany. The fear that all Jews in Europe are now in danger is magnified.

"We must warn the Danish Jews that they cannot be complacent. What is happening in Germany and their occupied countries will happen to them," says Charles.

"I agree," says Hans. "The Danes have been so good to us. We must stay here longer than expected to help them face the dangers ahead."

Charles has tried to contact Alana many times by telephone, but communications to The States has been difficult. He finally gets through. "Alana, my darling, I am safe in Denmark."

"Oh, thank God. Is Hans with you?"

"Yes. He is a fine young lad, and he has been very helpful in all our efforts getting here safely. We had some harrowing adventures, but the Danes are protecting us."

"When are you coming home? I miss you so much, and I am looking forward to seeing Hans again. It has been such a long time."

"I'm afraid our stay is going to be extended. We have much to do. I cannot guess how long it will take to accomplish our goals."

"My love, what goals are you talking about?"

"I cannot say over the phone. You never know who might be listening. All I can say is our escape plan has greatly expanded."

Suddenly there is a crackle in the line. Charles speaks louder into the receiver, "Hello, hello, Alana can you hear me?" She cannot—the phone line has gone dead.

CHAPTER 7

April---September 1939

Charles and Anne Lindbergh move back to the United States. They rent a home by the sea on Long Island. His pro-Nazi and anti-Semitic views grow even stronger.

In the months before the start of World War II, Lindbergh's writings and speeches are hateful diatribes emphasizing his prejudicial stance. In one particularly outrageous radio address, he outlines his pro-Nazi sympathies and then blames what he calls the "Jewish-controlled media" for distortions and exaggerations of what is going on in Germany.

His continuing belief in eugenics is equally bizarre and Nazi-influenced. Many times over, he opines that the breeding and survival of "The White Race" is crucial and even more important than European democracy. Most Americans are aghast at his lunacy, but some are inappropriately swayed by them. Those who share his views still consider him a hero because of his past deeds. But a small majority now see him for what he is—a foolish bigot and traitor.

World War II begins when Germany invades Poland on September 1, 1939. Hitler and his generals have been planning this attack for years with their gigantic military buildup. Britain and France declare against Germany two days later. The world fears the death and destruction that surely will follow.

Lindbergh now has additional fuel for his soapbox rantings. He often repeats his quest for American isolation from the conflict, blaming any support for the war on the "Jewish influence of the press". His speeches often include the following quotes:

"If our people were only told the truth, they would see why we should not enter the War."

"We must be free of the distractions of European powers."

"We should not let the passions of other peoples lead our country to destruction."

These comments and others like them cause Franklin Roosevelt to say, "I am completely convinced that Lindbergh is a Nazi."

****

"What do you think of your *hero* now Alaine? With the world at war, he continues to preach his bigotry. He is blind to the atrocities the Nazis are inflicting," says Charles.

"Grandpa, I only wish everyone in my class can hear the truths you are speaking."

"I have tried to relate to you just the facts as I remember them, but I am not a history book, and it was fifty years ago. Some of the quotes and the timeline of events might be a little off, but I think I have gotten the point across—Lindbergh was a bad, evil man."

"Yes, Grandpa—that is now obvious to me."

CHAPTER 8

April---May 1940

The German military march through Europe continues. After invading Poland, the Nazis accomplish the same in Norway, Belgium, The Netherlands, Luxemburg, France, and Denmark.

Little to no resistance is met anywhere and all these countries are quickly occupied and dominated by the German forces. Hundreds of thousands of Jews suffer capture and eventual shipment to concentration camps in Germany, Austria, and Poland.

The occupation of Denmark in 1940 is unique. Due to the need for Danish agriculture to supply meat, butter, and other staples, the treatment afforded the Danes is quite benign compared to other occupied countries.

Political independence and the throne of King Charles X are retained. The parliament, court system, and the press are allowed to continue as before. Denmark is considered by German propaganda, because of its loyal cooperation, to be a "Model Protectorate".

The "Jewish Issue" in Denmark presents the most imposing problem for the German regime. The most hardline of them want to continue their crusade against Jews, but ultimately more moderate officials get their way (at least for the time being). Any implementation of their typical cruel actions will wait.

For over two years, Charles Levine and his followers have been living comfortably in and around Esbjerg thanks to the generosity of the Danes. Friendships and romances have occurred. Charles has been living in Dr. Karl Baum's guest cottage and has grown close to Karl. Hans and Frida's relationship has evolved into a loving romance, and Faye and Karl's son, Jonas, have been dating seriously. The occupation by Germany, though, has everyone worried.

On a beautiful spring day, Karl and Charles walk in Karl's garden. "It appears to me that we can continue our peaceful existence here, even with the German presence," says Karl.

"I am not so sure," says Charles. "I know what the Germans are capable of. Now they are like sleeping bears looking gentle but give them a little poke and their claws and fangs will be exposed to present a ferocious foe."

Karl considers Charles' thoughts. "You may be right. What are you proposing to do?"

"I think we must seriously plan our escape from Denmark. It is only a matter of time before the Germans show their true colors against us Jews. We must be prepared."

It does not take long for an incident to occur, which proves Charles' fear to be correct. Three days later, Faye and Jonas are walking hand in hand along a quiet street, minding their own business. Two German soldiers approach them. "Hey, Jew boy, is this your Jewish whore?" one of them yells out.

Jonas answers politely, "Please watch what you say. This is my girlfriend."

The other soldier raises his rifle and strikes Jonas in the head with its butt. Jonas falls to the ground, bleeding. "Don't talk back to us, you Jew pig. Your days of freedom are numbered."

Faye bends down to help Jonas. The first soldier kicks her in the ass. She topples over on top of Jonas. The soldiers both laugh hysterically at the sight.

Faye raises her fist in anger and yells, "God damn you bastards."

Jonas stops her from saying any more. "Faye, let it go." The soldiers walk away still laughing.

That evening, Charles, Karl, Hans, Frida, Faye, and Jonas meet. Charles leads the discussion, "The time has come to leave Denmark."

"I concur," says Hans. "We have overstayed our welcome. Now that the Germans are here, it will not stay peaceful much longer."

Frida and Faye are quick to agree with Charles and Hans.

Jonas, with a bandage on his head, puts his arms around Faye. "If you are leaving, I am going with you," he says.

Karl listens intensely to the conversation. He is conflicted. "I cannot blame you all for your fears. But one stupid incident should not determine life-changing decisions. The Germans promised that Jews can co-exist in Denmark safely. We should not be thinking only of the people in this room. We have 8000 Jews here we must worry about."

"Karl, even more of a reason to plan ahead," says Charles. "We will implement our original escape plan. If successful, it will give all Jews a blueprint to eventually follow."

"I can see I will not be able to dissuade you. I wish you all good luck---I will not be joining you. The well-being of all my patients and my neighboring Jews are what I must be concerned about. Jonas, my son, if you think it best to go, I will not stand in your way. I love you and will pray every day for your safety," says Karl.

Jonas kisses his father. "And I for yours," he says.

"What is our next step?" asks Frida.

Charles answers, "We will move our entire group to Copenhagen to be close to the sea and the Swedish border. There we will join forces with the Danish underground and plot out our next moves. We will pack and leave in two days."

Karl takes out a pen and scribbles a name and an address on a pad. "This is the man you should see in Copenhagen. He is the person who can help you."

Charles looks at the name. He is pleasantly surprised.

CHAPTER 9

June 1940

Neils Bohr is the most famous and respected Dane in the world. His contributions in physics earn him the Nobel Prize in 1922. His theories on atomic structure and quantum mechanics are critical revelations to those fields of study. He is considered one of the most brilliant minds of his time. He is also a Jew, living in Copenhagen.

To Charles Levine, it is a fortuitous choice that such an influential person as Neils Bohr should be the name given to him by Karl Baum as the person best equipped to assist him.

Charles arrives at a meeting at Neils Bohr's residence the day after getting to Copenhagen. "Mr. Bohr, it is such a pleasure to meet you, sir."

Neils has been briefed on the purpose of the meeting. "Please call me Neils and stop with the sirs. We are both just two Jewish men looking for solutions. I am working with the Danish Underground to help in any way I can. I am fortunate that my name can open doors."

"Let me inform you of the gist of our plans. I have fifty Jews from Germany who are trying to escape to Sweden. As you are aware, Sweden is a neutral country in The War. The Germans do not wish to interfere with that neutrality and will not disturb Jews who reside there. We hope that we can cross the sea into Sweden undetected and be allowed by the Swedish government to stay."

"What you're planning is risky and will be difficult to achieve, as I am sure you realize."

"I certainly do. But, with the help of the underground resistance, of which you are an important part, I am confident our escape can be achieved. In addition, it is my feeling, it will not be long before the Nazis renew their nefarious ways and bring danger to all Danish Jews. If executed properly, our escape plan can be used similarly for all 8000 Jews one day."

"I share your fear that the Nazis will soon abandon their current position on Danish Jews. We should be prepared for that eventuality. I will help. What do you want me to do?"

Neils and Charles continue to talk for hours. A difficult scenario is put into place.

****

"Grandpa, more than just trying to save fifty German Jews, you have a role in trying to save 8000 Danish Jews. Is that correct?" Alaine asks.

"You are getting ahead of the story, but yes, my dear, that was the goal," answers Charles.

"While you were away from your home and wife for so long, trying to save so many people, what was Charles Lindbergh doing?"

"He was trying his best to isolate America from any involvement in the war by continuing his anti-Semitic rhetoric. Let me explain how he was able to do this on a large scale."

"In September of 1940, the America First Committee, a group dedicated to keeping America out of The War is formed. This isolationist group is headed by the infamous antisemite, Henry Ford, and among its members are Joseph Kennedy Sr. (another well-known antisemite), future president Gerald Ford, and WW! flying ace Eddie Rickenbacker. Lindbergh eventually becomes its lead spokesman and loudest voice. In front of thousands of people at Madison Square Garden in New York and

Soldier Field in Chicago, he loudly preaches his beliefs that the U.S. should not help our European allies. Millions listen to his speech on the radio.

His arguments include statements that German policies against Jews are none of America's concern. A constant theme is that the survival of Germany is preferable to a Soviet alliance. He even proposes that the United States enter into a neutrality agreement with Germany.

Many fall for his foolishness. Franklin Roosevelt repeats his opinion that "Lindbergh is a traitor."

CHAPTER 10

July 1940

Captain Franz Schmitt is on a vendetta to find and capture Charles, Hans, and their group. He is overcome with guilt that they were able to escape from Berlin on his watch. Through the torture of Emil, the evening before his murder, he knows that fifty Jews fled to Denmark. He is especially committed to finding the woman who killed the border guard, Horace Schmitt, who by happenstance was his nephew. The other guard at the scene has identified the killer as a tall, beautiful woman with long blond hair.

Schmitt is frustrated in his efforts—for over two years his search has been in vain. The Danish citizens have been too proficient at hiding the refugees. He acknowledges that to continue his search, he will need some useful inside clues. Fortunately for him, suddenly he gets some.

A German spy, living in Esbjerg, is a patient of Dr. Karl Baum. Hiding behind a partially closed door, he overhears a conversation between Dr. Baum and his nurse. From what he is able to hear, he gleans that both Dr. Baum and his nurse have been harboring Jews from

Germany at their homes. He learns that they and others are now on the move, headed for Copenhagen.

The news is relayed to Berlin—Schmitt is elated. He asks his commanding officer for permission to assemble thirty soldiers to go to Copenhagen and capture the refugees.

The General responds to the request, "Captain, give it up. You lost fifty Jews two years ago because of your incompetence. We are now killing thousands of them, fifty more is not going to make a difference."

"Sir, I beg to differ. This group defied our laws and, in the process, killed one of our men, my nephew. We must make an example of them. We will not tolerate such behavior."

"Schmitt, you are being overly emotional due to your failures and the fact that they killed a relative of yours. Everyone around the world knows quite well our tolerance for Jews is very limited." The General laughs at his obvious understatement.

"Sir, but…"

"Captain, do not interrupt me!" The General spits out. "I must remind you, we have promised the Danish government, we will not interfere with their Jews."

"Sir, these are not Danish Jews, they are German Jews living in Denmark, illegally. We have every right to capture them and punish them with the justice they deserve."

"Captain, I give you credit for your persistence. I will relent—you can go to Copenhagen, but only with three soldiers. We cannot spare any more men for a foolish escapade. You will have to make do."

Schmitt is disappointed. The small size of his force will make his plan more difficult, but he has no choice. "Thank you, sir. We leave tomorrow."

CHAPTER 11

July 1940

Neils Bohr takes the train to Sweden to meet with the King of Sweden, King Gustav V. He is fulfilling his promise to Charles to try to convince The King to allow passage into his country.

He meets The King at his palace. They have talked before, but only on social occasions. "Your Highness, thank you for meeting with me on such short notice." He kisses the King's ring.

"I will get right to the point. I require a favor. Fifty Jews request asylum in your country. Will you be willing to allow them? I ask only because of its urgency and importance."

The King responds, "Mr. Bohr, your reputation and accomplishments speak for themselves. You are not only a great scientist, but a great humanitarian. But what you are asking for is a lot. Jews from all over Europe crave refugee status. Our country cannot accommodate the masses that want to escape German brutality. We have quota limits for that purpose that have already been filled."

"Let me explain more fully why I ask for this favor. The fifty friends I speak of are German refugees. They have been hiding in Denmark for two years. Present conditions force them to want to move now to safer grounds, namely Sweden. They face certain death otherwise."

"Are you seeking asylum for yourself?"

"Not at present, but soon all Danish Jews' lives, including my own, will be in danger of facing German bigotry. Their extermination will be Hitler's goal."

"I am fully aware of Hitler's intentions. He is a maniacal despot."

"That is exactly why the survival of this group is so important. Their success will be a guide and an inspiration for all Danish Jews."

"I have heard enough; You make an imposing case. To maintain my country's neutrality, I cannot officially say or support any conduct that might be considered favoritism to another country or group. I must say this as my country's Head of State."

The King takes Neils aside and whispers into his ear, *"But your cause is just."*

Neils comprehends The King's message—its meaning is clear. "I understand your position."

"Good, now go in peace and God-willing, all will work out for the best."

Neils returns to Copenhagen and meets with Charles. "It is a go. Make your plans to go to Sweden."

"Did The King agree to that?" asks Charles.

"Not exactly. There will be no official statement of approval or tacit assistance, but no one should stand in your way. That is the best I could do."

"It is more than enough. Your help is greatly appreciated. Fifty people owe their lives to you."

"I did my little part. The rest is up to you."

CHAPTER 12

August 1940

The nearest point between Denmark and Sweden is across an area of the sea known as *The Sound* from Helsingor, Denmark to Helsingborg, Sweden. The distance is only two and a half miles and in calm seas and a good boat the crossing should only take about forty minutes. It is this route that Charles has chosen to take to Sweden, but he needs a boat.

Otto Anderson is the captain of *The Gerda III,* a small boat that can seat twenty passengers. The vessel is used by The Danish Lighthouse Service for normal trips twice a day to the lighthouse in the middle of *The Sound.*

"Otto, can I persuade you to detour to Sweden on two of your trips with a few passengers?" asks Charles at the dock where the boat is anchored.

Otto is a wise, old sea captain who has been crossing *The Sound* for over forty years. He knows exactly what Charles is asking. "Oh, you're smuggling some Jews to Sweden. How many are we talking about?" he asks.

"Twenty-five persons per trip."

"The boat can only handle twenty people comfortably, but for the right price, I can be persuaded to jam a few more heads on board. I want one thousand Kroner per person."

"That is a steep price," responds Charles.

"Yes, it is, but I suspect you are asking me to avoid some nasty Germans that might be on the lookout for you. I am taking a big risk!"

When Charles left the United States, he had a substantial amount of funds due to the generosity of Jewish charities. After two years that sum has dwindled considerably to only a small amount remaining. But Charles knows he has no choice. "Captain, you have yourself a deal. In a few days, we ship out. I will notify you when I know the exact day." The two men shake hands.

As he walks away from the dock, Charles worries, *"Now I have to figure out how to get everyone to the boat, undetected by the Germans, and where do I get 50,000 Kroner?"*

Charles gathers Hans, Frida, Fay, and Jonas together to go over the details of the escape plan. "The boat we are taking is in Helsingor, about twenty-eight miles from Copenhagen. Hans and I will arrange transportation to just short of town. We will split up into two groups and walk one mile through the dense woods. Everyone will be allowed to bring only one piece of luggage with them. There is an old church, just beyond the woods—that is where we will reunite. From there it is a short walk to the boat. Then, we are off to Sweden. Any questions?"

Frida asks, "Why so complicated? Why don't we go straight to the dock?"

"My biggest concern is that the Germans will be looking for us. They have spies everywhere. That is why we are splitting into groups. If one group is confronted, at least the other one should be safe. Jonas and Faye will lead the first group with ten others and scout the area. Frida, Hans, and I will follow behind with the rest. Jonas, you will advise the others of our plans."

"Sounds good," says Jonas. "When do we leave?"

"In two days. We arrive at dusk; walk through the woods during the night; stay overnight at the church; cross the sea in the morning; and arrive in Sweden one hour later. Simple, right?"

In their hearts, everyone knows it will not be that easy.

Franz Schmitt and his three soldiers arrive in Copenhagen. At the same time as Charles is giving his instructions to his crew, Schmitt is doing the same to his. He has been briefed by the spies and is getting updates routinely. "We are going to stake out the woods near the town of Helsingor. That is the most likely place where the Jews will try to cross into Sweden. We leave today. There is an old church near the woods—we will stay there tonight."

CHAPTER 13

August 1940

Charles calls Dr. Baum. "Karl, I need your help."

"Dear friend, we have come this far together—if you need something I will be there for you. The train to Copenhagen leaves shortly. I will be there in about three hours. We will meet at Bohr's house," Baum replies.

"Thank you."

Charles and Hans are nervous, as well as they should be. The last final phases of a plan are always the most difficult. They wait for Dr. Baum at Niels Bohr's home. He is one hour late.

"I'm so sorry for being late—the train was delayed," Karl says as he comes through the door. Without any hesitation, he asks, "What is it you need?"

Hans answers, "We need transportation for our people to Helsingor."

"That is no problem. We can get you a bus. But you didn't get me here to only ask for that. What else is there?"

Charles now speaks, "The people of Denmark and your resistance movement have been so kind to us, we hate to impose on you further, but we are desperate. We need 50,000 kroner to pay for our passage."

"That is a lot of money, but we have many wealthy Danes, Jews, and non-Jews, who are committed to our resistance against the Germans. We have helped you for two years—we are not going to stop now. You will get your funds, but I need two days to accumulate it."

"Of course, I will delay our departure until the funds are secured. You are too kind, thank you," says Charles.

"There is one more thing. We need guns," says Hans.

"I worry about the safety of your group and especially the safety of my son. You are right to think of the dangers that might lie ahead. The need to defend yourself is legitimate. We will supply the weapons you request."

Before saying their goodbyes, Hans asks Charles a question. "Should I tell the group about the delay in our departure?"

Charles answers quickly. "No, to be safe, let's keep it quiet."

Hans, Charles, and Karl all hug. Karl says, "Now go with God. "I will stay here until I know you are all safely on the shores of Sweden."

CHAPTER 14

August 1940

The old church in Helsingor has not been in use for over ten years—and it looks it. The steps leading to the front door are broken; the floorboards inside are rotted away; and the roof has numerous holes. To make matters worse, horrid odors from the feces left by raccoons and stray dogs permeate throughout.

These are the conditions that Captain Schmitt and his men find upon their arrival. "I know it is a mess, but we will only be here for two days," Schmitt says. "Sergeant, have your men clean up as best they can. Afterward, go on patrol into the woods."

"Yes sir," Sergeant Schultz replies.

Three hours later, Schultz and the other two soldiers return to the church. "There is nothing out there, but trees, overgrown brush, and a lot of mosquitos," the Sergeant reports.

"No, I did not expect there would be anyone. The Jews are not scheduled to arrive until tomorrow, but I thought it wise for you to get the lay of the land. We can turn in for the night now. Make yourself comfortable."

The Sergeant laughs to himself at the suggestion. "Yes sir, we will try."

The next day, Schmitt and his men wander into the town. They walk past the dock where all the fishing and sightseeing boats are anchored. "This is where they will try to escape from. Monitor anything that looks suspicious," Schmitt instructs.

Captain Anderson observes the Germans from afar. He is concerned, but not fearful. He continues to prepare his boat for that day's trips.

After four hours of doing mostly nothing other than just walking around, Sergeant Schultz asks for a break in his duties. "Sir, the men and I would like to go to the pub down the street for a few beers. Is that alright?"

"Yes, that is a good idea. I think I'll join you," Schmitt replies, also bored.

In Copenhagen, Charles and his entire group spend a leisurely day. All fifty of his people have been residing comfortably at the homes of the resistance members.

Charles and Hans have a chat over coffee. "I purposely have not told the group what day we are leaving for Helsingor. As of now, they think it is today. Let's keep them thinking that," says Charles.

"Why the subterfuge?" asks Hans.

"Our group is staying at about thirty homes of supposedly loyal resistance members. But the odds are there is a mole among them who is spying for the Germans in one of those homes. We should keep our secrets as long as possible."

"Very wise!"

After getting a bite to eat and imbibing two beers each at the pub, Schmitt orders his men back to the church. "Tonight, we can expect the refugees. We must be prepared to fight."

"We will be ready," says Schultz.

At nightfall, the three soldiers march back into the woods. Schmitt follows closely behind. They spend the whole night suffering in the woods. Mosquitos are plentiful and wet, uncomfortable conditions abound with no sighting of refugees.

At daylight, the four Germans drudge back to the church. "Sir, if you don't mind, I would like to speak up?" asks Shultz.

"Yes, Sergeant, what is it?"

"Your intel must be faulty. There is no sign of your Jews."

"I am aware. We must have gotten the days mixed up. My spies are usually very reliable. I am sure tonight we will find them."

"I hope you're right. The men are getting tired of living under these conditions."

"Sergeant, you are getting very close to being insubordinate. Another word from you and I'll send you to the front lines and you'll see what bad conditions are really like."

The Sergeant walks away quietly, but convinced they are on a fool's mission.

Charles and his group spend another leisurely summer day in Copenhagen. Many explore all the beautiful sights of the city. Hans stays behind in the home he is living in. At noon, a courier appears at the house. He carries a large satchel and an envelope.

He rushes to see Charles sitting on a nearby park bench. "I have received the funds and the weapons. We are ready to go."

"Great, the bus arrives in the morning. We leave for Helsingor tomorrow at 9 p.m. I will inform Captain Anderson we can cross the seas the following day."

"Should I tell everyone?" asks Hans.

"No, wait until tomorrow. We can't be cautious enough."

That night, the German soldiers again stake out the woods. Schmitt stays behind in the church, waiting for news. Still, there is no sign of the Jews. It is another long, boring, and uncomfortable night for the soldiers.

The next day Charles gathers his group together at 6 pm after a quiet day of nervous anticipation in Copenhagen. He finally tells everyone about the departure plans. "We leave in three hours but do not tell anyone. We must keep our secrets if we are to be successful." At 9 pm they all board the bus.

At the church, at that same time, Schmitt orders his men, "Ok, back in the woods. This should be it."

Sergeant Schultz slowly rises. Under his breath, he says to himself, *"I've heard that before."* He and the other two soldiers walk out the door.

"I am sick and tired of going into those stinging woods on this idiotic wild search for some presumed refugees for this crazy Captain. Guys, I'm going to the pub." The other soldiers gladly follow their sergeant.

CHAPTER 15

August 1940

The passengers sit in silence throughout the bus ride. All are contemplating what the next few hours will bring. Survival is their only goal.

At about 10 p.m., the bus pulls up to the edge of the woods adjoining Helsingor. "Ok, this is our stop," Charles says, trying to make light of their situation.

Faye picks out ten men from the group. She chooses the biggest and strongest. "Men, you will be with Jonas and me. We are going first. The walk will be about one mile through the woods. Stay close and be careful. Germans can be anywhere along the route."

Jonas hands guns to four of the men. "I hope you know how to use these," he says, quite sure they do not. They start walking forward. Charles, Hans, Frida, and the others wait behind for ten minutes and then take another route.

It is a difficult walk, through dense brush with only the moonlight to see by. Both groups stop frequently to gain their bearings and to take a breath. Nerves are more the strain than the physical effort.

Going slowly, it takes about an hour for Faye and Jonas to reach their destination, so far without incident. Jonas whispers to the group, "I can see the church. We are almost there." He steps on a dead tree branch; the sound carries in the quiet night air.

Captain Schmitt, alone in the church, but ever alert, hears something. He grabs his revolver and walks to the edge of the trees. "Schultz, are you there? I think I heard something," he whispers. There is no reply. "Schultz, Schultz, I need you." Still no reply.

Schmitt advances slowly. He sees the outline of a man. He hides behind a large tree, waiting like a hungry animal ready to pounce on its prey. A woman now appears in his sight and then about ten others. He is badly outnumbered. Assuming the man and woman are the leaders of the group, he calculates that if he can subdue those two, the others will back down.

Schmitt waits until they are close to him, no more than three yards away. He shoots once and then again. Both bullets find their target. Jonas is hit in his shoulder and his leg and immediately falls to the ground. Schmitt quickly jumps up and grabs Faye around her neck before she can react. His gun is pointed at her head. "Drop your guns or she dies," he yells out to the others, terrified at what they just saw.

"Do as he says," Faye yells out, fearful, but somehow also bravely. The others drop their weapons. Faye looks down at Jonas lying helplessly on the ground. Despite her predicament, her concern for him dominates her thoughts.

Now in total control of the situation, Schmitt kicks all the guns to the side and ties Faye to the nearest tree. The others move sheepishly back. "Well, it looks like I have found the beautiful, blond-haired girl who killed my nephew." He points his gun once again at her head.

"No, no, it was not me. You have the wrong person," Faye yells out.

"I'm sorry dear, I got a very good description from the other guard at the scene. It was definitely you. Prepare to die!"

From their location, about thirty yards away, Hans and Frida have heard the gunshots. They rush forward to observe the scene and kneel in the bushes to hide. Hans is quick to comprehend what must be done. "Give him hell, Frida---fire away," Hans instructs in a whisper.

Suddenly, a rifle shot rings out from out of the darkness. The bullet strikes Schmitt on his arm, just above his wrist. His gun falls to the ground, and he writhes uncontrollably in pain. The four men quickly retrieve their fallen guns.

Frida lowers her rifle, stands up, and proudly exclaims, "She is right, it was me who killed your nephew."

Hans moves forward and hits Schmitt over the top of his head with the back of his gun. He unties Faye. Schmitt, now groggy, and with four guns pointing at him, realizes his mistake. "There are two of you."

"Now, you got it, you stupid Nazi. I am so proud of my sister. Her sharp-shooting ability is dead-on," says Faye.

Faye then bends down to tend to Jonas. "He is alive. The bullets look like they went clear through, but we must care for his wounds. Get me some bandages."

Jonas awakes. "Did I miss anything?" he asks.

Charles and the others arrive at the scene just minutes later. He is shocked and elated at what he sees. "It looks like you kids have everything under control. Tie him to the tree, and let's decide what we should do with him."

Everyone yells out, "Kill him!"

Charles tries to calm the crowd. "I think it is only fair to first have a trial and then kill him." Everyone laughs.

Charles acts as the prosecutor and starts an interrogation of Schmitt. "Did you kill Fran and Fredrick Weinberg?"

To his credit, Schmitt answers honestly, "Yes, but please have mercy on me."

"I will continue," says Charles. "Did you order the execution of Emil Gutmer?"

"Yes, I did." Schmitt lowers his head.

"One final question. Did you have Josef Rudolph and twenty others sent to concentration camps?"

"Yes, yes." In desperation, he pleads, "Please forgive me. I was just taking orders."

Charles looks to the entire group. "Jury, how do you find the defendant?"

"Guilty!" They all yell.

"The jury has given their verdict. There will be no forgiveness for this man's hideous crimes. The sentence is for death."

Frida steps up first. "I suffered remorse when I killed your nephew, but there will be no tears shed this time. I now know Nazis are pure evil. For all the people you sent to concentration camps to suffer and die, including my dear brother, Josef, this justice is for you." She shoots Schmitt in the stomach—he screams.

Faye now stands in front of the defendant. She spits in his eye and shoots him in the chest—Schmitt screams louder. "That is for Emil, may he rest in peace."

Now it is Hans' turn. "For me and my sister, Alana, I send you to hell for murdering my parents. May the memories of my dear mother, Fran, and my beloved father, Fredrick, remain always in our hearts. He shoots Schmitt twice in the head. There are no screams--the Nazi is dead.

At the pub in town, Schultz and his men are on their fifth round of drinks, unaware and uncaring about what has transpired in the woods.

CHAPTER 16

August 1940

The body of Schmitt is left to rot among the trees. Hans leads the group in walking to the church. Once inside, they rejoice—their journey is almost at an end.

Charles notices the gear left by the Germans. "Do not celebrate too soon, it appears that the Nazi soldiers were using this filthy place as their outpost. There is enough stuff here for four men. We must remain vigilant in looking out for the other three. Hans, pick four men to stand guard throughout the night."

Frida and Faye look after Jonas. He is conscious and feeling a little better, although still in a lot of pain. Fortunately, they have packed antibiotics, painkillers, and bandages in case of injuries. Jonas whispers, "You girls are great. You showed that stinking Nazi what brave Jewish women can do."

Faye takes his hand in hers and kisses it gently but realizes that is not enough affection for the man she loves. She gives Jonas a big kiss on his lips. "Darling, I think it's time we tell the group about our plans."

"Yes dear, that is a good idea, do that," Jonas says as he falls asleep.

Faye stands up in front of the whole group. "Listen up everyone, I have a big announcement—Jonas and I are getting married." Everyone cheers.

With a big smile on her face, Faye continues her speech, "Jonas proposed two weeks ago under a moonlit sky, and, of course, I accepted." Everyone cheers again. "Thank you for your support, but there is more that I must say."

Faye continues, "We have decided that we will not be going on to Sweden with you. We are staying in Denmark. Jonas and I want to be with his family, and at his temple for this joyous occasion. And now, with his injuries, it is best that he stays here to be treated by his father. We love you all and wish you only the best in your new home." Simultaneously, tears of joy and sadness run down her face.

Frida rushes up to Faye. There is a certain bond between twins that cannot be denied. They hug so passionately that their bodies appear to almost intertwine.

Frida's emotions are conflicted. "I'm so happy for you, but we have never been apart. How am I going to survive without you?"

Faye tries to make light of their impending separation. "I'm sure you'll manage somehow." They hug one more time. "I promise you, someday we will be together again."

After everyone comes over to Faye to wish her good fortune, Faye takes Charles aside for a private chat. "I want to thank you personally for all that you have done for me, Jonas, and all the others. Without you, most of us would not have survived."

Charles interrupts her speech, "Don't thank me yet, we still have hurdles to climb before we are safely in Sweden."

"I'm not worried. You got us this far--the next small part of the journey that remains should be easy," she says. "I love you and will never forget you." She fondly kisses him on his forehead. Charles blushes.

"There is another reason why Jonas and I decided to stay."

"I sort of guessed that."

"The Jewish Danes will need our help, when the Nazis come after them, and we all know that day will come. Jonas has a lot of Jewish friends and family in Denmark and the experiences we have had in avoiding the Nazis will be useful for their escape. We will warn and guide them the entire time as part of the resistance movement."

"Your plan is admirable. The Danes deserve the help you two will give. You will be in my prayers."

The two of them sit silently for a minute. "Now, it is time for sleep. It has been a long day and we need to leave early tomorrow."

"Yes, Jonas and I will grab a taxi to Copenhagen at daylight."

"I probably will not see you that early." He holds Faye's hand. "Goodbye, good luck and may your future be filled with happiness."

CHAPTER 17

August 1940

At 8 a.m., Hans yells out, "Everyone up. This is our big day. We're off to Sweden. Please try your best to dress like Danes going on a sightseeing trip in *The Sound*."

Charles adds, "We will split into two groups. I will lead the first group and Hans and Frida will lead the second one. Hans, you will wait here about ninety minutes until the boat returns for its second trip."

Charles and his group walk towards the dock. As they do so, they pass the three German soldiers dead asleep on the lawn of the pub, not yet recovered from their night of reverie. "Be quiet everyone. We don't want to wake these sleeping beauties," he cautions his followers.

They arrive at the dock where Captain Otto stands smiling on his boat. "Is everyone ready for a lovely day on *The Sound?*" he asks.

They all cheer, quietly.

Charles hands Otto 50,000 Kroner. The captain's smile grows even wider. "Let's get going quickly—three Nazis are sleeping on the shore," Charles warns Otto.

As the last passengers board the boat, the Germans start to stir from their slumber. Still hungover, they stumble to stand up. In the distance, through blurred eyes, Sergeant Schultz sees the many passengers on a small boat. He is suspicious. "Who goes there?" he yells out.

Otto ignores the question and starts to guide the boat away from the dock.

Schultz again yells out, "Stop, stop, I need to question you people." He draws his gun and fires a warning shot into the air.

Otto remains calm, but sighs to Charles, "This is what I was afraid of."

Charles responds, "Just keep going. In the shape they are in, I don't think they could hit an elephant standing right in front of them. Also, I have people on the shore who will take care of this little inconvenience."

Hans hears the gunshot. "Frida, grab your gun and come with me. I think there is trouble on the dock."

Hans sizes up the situation. The Germans are talking to themselves, apparently confused as to what to do. Hans and Frida surround them from behind. They point their guns at the Germans.

Frida is comfortable with this confrontation. She speaks sternly and confidently, "Nazi pigs, drop your weapons!"

Sergeant Schultz and his men slowly turn around. Schultz is not stupid—he knows when he is beaten. "Men, do as she says." All their guns fall to the ground.

Hans now takes charge. "Sergeant, your captain is dead, and if you give us any trouble you soon will be too. Your job is over here, but this is a good day, and I am feeling charitable. If you do what I say, I will spare your lives. I want you to start running as fast as you can into the woods, and don't look back for an hour. Do you understand me?"

"Yes sir," Shultz whines respectfully.

"Ok, now go!" The three Germans take off into the woods as if they are running a marathon at the Olympics.

Frida and Hans smile, their day has started well. They wave towards their friends with their arms held high, as the boat slowly disappears from sight. Charles and twenty-five others (including Captain Otto) wave back.

The seas remain calm as Charles looks to the sky, contemplating what he and his friends have accomplished. He smiles broadly.

In surprisingly quick fashion, the boat pulls up to the dock of Helsingborg in Sweden. A Swedish sailor dressed in an all-white formal uniform greets the passengers. "Charles Levine, we have been expecting you. Welcome to Sweden."

Two hours later, Hans, Frida, and the rest successfully arrive. They get the same greeting.

****

"That must have been a great feeling, after all this time, to finally be on safe ground," says Alaine.

"You have no idea," replies Charles. "I felt like the weight of the world was lifted from my shoulders. But, as I was to find out, my problems were far from over."

Who is Charles Levine?

PART VII: THE SMUGGLER

CHAPTER 1

August 1940

The first thing Charles does while on Swedish soil is call Alana. "Hello darling, we made it. We are in Sweden. I'll be coming home soon."

Alana yells out a screech, "Wonderful, when?"

"It's not so much about the when—it's about the how. I'm working on my means of transportation."

"And my brother—how is he?"

"He is fine and looking forward to seeing you again. He will be coming with a companion."

"A companion? You mean a girlfriend?"

"Yes, a lovely woman named Frida. Hans, Frida, and her sister exacted revenge on the murderer of your parents. We will tell you the full story when we return."

"Charles, I love you so much. I can't wait to see you."

"It won't be long now. I must tie up some loose ends. I will call you again when I know the details of our arrival. Goodbye for now my sweet girl."

The second thing Charles needs to do is send a telegram to Bill Donovan:

Wild One, we made it to Sweden. We are in Helsingborg. Now get me out of here. There will be three of us going to America. Please make arrangements asap. I have been away from my wife and my country for too long.

Regards, The Aviator

The final piece of business for his first day is the most important and the hardest. He needs to find places to live for fifty German refugees. Although he got them to the place he promised, he still feels responsible. They must find shelter.

Charles and Hans head to the Swedish Department of Health and Welfare office. "We are refugees from Denmark and Germany. We need housing for about fifty people. What can you do for us?" Charles asks of the woman behind the desk.

The woman looks frazzled. "Do you have any idea how many refugees I am trying to find housing for?" Before Charles can attempt to guess, the woman answers her own question. "I'll tell you—too many. For reasons unknown to me, you and your group were allowed into this country. You must have friends in high places. But that does not mean I have housing for you. Your group must fend for themselves. Temporarily, but only for a few days, they can stay in a gymnasium that we have set up for that purpose. After that, they are on their own. If that means living on the street, so be it."

Charles, Hans, and Frida hope to be gone before the end of those three days. For the fifty others—it will be a problem. But that is the life to be expected by refugees in a new country during wartime.

Charles advises the group needing housing of the issues they face. Still giddy about their successful arrival in Sweden, they do not appear to be troubled. In fact, they are all celebrating at a local bar.

A spokesman for the group approaches Charles, "Do not worry, my friend—you have done enough. Please, we are Jews--we are a resourceful force, and we will find our way. You can be sure of that."

Charles smiles. He is relieved. His job is over.

At the end of this long day, Charles receives a telegram from Wild Bill:

Well done. I never doubted your efforts for a minute. A plane arrives tomorrow in Helsingborg to transport you and your two friends to The States. You are deserving of a hero's welcome.

See you there, Wild One

But more trouble looms. A hero's welcome is not in the cards.

CHAPTER 2

August 1940

There is no airport in Helsingborg. For planes needing to land near the city, the best they can do is an open field about two miles outside of town. It is here that Charles, Hans, and Frida wait to be transported to the United States.

After two hours, a plane appears, coming out of the West. It lands forty yards from where they are standing. Hans has taken a huge interest in aviation. He recognizes the type of plane, "that is a military transport single-engine plane. Its full name is the Fairchild C-61 Forwarder. It seats four passengers."

Frida is appropriately nervous. She responds, "I don't care what it is, as long as it stays in the air."

Charles, the experienced flyer, tries to allay her fears. "Don't you worry, I can tell that is a solid aircraft. I have flown in much worse."

The plane rolls to a stop and the pilot exits. To Charles' surprise, it is a familiar face. "Clarence, my friend, it is so nice to see you again."

217

Charles makes the introductions, "Hans, Frida meet Clarence Chamberlin, my old buddy from my aviation days. Clarence was my pilot for our record-setting flight to Berlin back in 1927."

Clarence responds, "It is my pleasure to meet you. I can assure you this flight will be a hell of a lot smoother than that one."

"Besides flying old men like me back home, what have you been doing since we were last together?" asks Charles.

"I've been training young studs how to fly. These kid pilots are a raw breed, but if and when we get into this war, the U.S. Air Force will be ready. But enough about me, I understand you have been a busy boy. Tell me about your exploits."

"They are not important—we will talk later. Right now, I just want to get to the good old U.S. of A. Let's get out of here."

"I see nothing has changed—you're still giving instructions. But, as always, you are right. All aboard everyone," Clarence orders.

Neither Frida nor Hans has ever been on an airplane. Hans is excited. Frida is scared.

"I can't wait. This will be the thrill of a lifetime," says Hans.

"I have faced Germans at gunpoint, but I have never been so afraid," says Frida.

Clarence tries to calm her nerves. "Little lady, you are in the hands of a seasoned pro. Just sit back, buckle up, and enjoy the ride."

On takeoff, Frida lets out a primal scream. After fifteen minutes in the air, she starts breathing easier. She looks out the window and is amazed by the wonderous sight of the deep blue ocean below. She relaxes.

Charles moves into the cockpit to sit beside his friend. "What is the flight plan?" he asks.

"We fly Northwest for about ten hours when we will make a stop to refuel and rest in Greenland. Then, we head West to the Marine Air Terminal at LaGuardia Field in New York. Depending on the weather, the total flight time should be about twenty-two hours."

Charles takes a short nap of about an hour. When he awakes, he is in a talkative mood. "Clarence, I have read the news reports about the speeches of our old friend, Charles Lindbergh. What is going on with him?"

"Lindbergh is as arrogant and ignorant as ever. He preaches appeasement with the Germans whenever he can. He believes that you can reason with the Nazis. It seems to me that he even admires Hitler."

"Astonishing," says Charles.

"Our British and French friends need the U.S. to combat this evil empire, yet Lindbergh's isolationist policies persist. On top of that, he blames Jews for all the wrongs in the world. He is a madman. He sways a lot of people with his insane ideas."

Charles sits silently for a moment, thinking of a prudent response. "I have too much respect for the majority of Americans. They will wake up and realize what a monster Hitler is. They will see that Lindbergh is an idiotic puppet for a regime that is out to conquer the world with brutality and bigotry. In the last two years, I have personally witnessed their atrocities against humankind. They are horrific."

On the approach to Greenland, Clarence radios the airfield. "Fairchild C-61 requesting permission to land for refueling. Our approach is from the East."

The tower responds, "Fairchild C-61, you are cleared to land on runway Alpha 1."

Clarence loudly asks, "Charles, do you want to take over the controls and bring us down?"

220

In the back of the plane, Hans and Frida hear the question. Both have heard the stories about Charles' expertise or rather the lack thereof of landing an aircraft. They both yell out, "NO!"

"I was only kidding," says Clarence.

"Thank God," says Charles.

On land, Charles is surprised to see only U.S. military men on the tarmac. Greenland is normally an island, owned by Denmark. "Where are the Danes?" he asks Clarence.

"When Germany invaded Denmark, the U.S. took control of Greenland. It is an important island that they did not want to fall into German hands."

"Good to see that the U.S. is taking a least a small role in the conflict," says Charles.

Clarence takes a short nap, and Charles calls Alana telling her of their impending arrival in New York.

After refueling and dinner, Clarence and the three passengers are back in the air. "Nothing but clear skies ahead of us," says Clarence.

He is wrong. Not a half hour after giving that optimistic weather report the plane encounters severe turbulence. A sudden storm appears out of nowhere. The plane shakes violently; rain pelters down; lightning strikes are abundant.

Clarence remains calm. He even cracks a joke. "Charles, if we were in *The Columbia* in a storm like this, we would all be dead." Charles does not laugh-- he is nervous. He holds on tightly to the arm rails.

Frida screams. Hans tells Frida, "I love you. Say your prayers. I cannot believe, after all we have been through, this will be our fate."

Expertly, Clarence pulls hard on the throttle, lifting the plane higher. The engine sputters. "Don't worry," Clarence yells out so everyone can hear. "This is a strong plane. I'll get us through this."

Three minutes go by, it feels more like three hours, and the plane continues to shake out of control.

Suddenly, as quickly as the storm appeared, it is gone. Clarence has taken the plane above the clouds. He works the controls, and the engine recovers, first slowly, then in full force. The plane straightens out.

"You can all relax—we are out of danger. The rest of the trip should be in the clear," says Clarence.

"You said that before," chides Charles.

For the next ten hours, all is peaceful in flight. Charles tells Clarence of all his adventures in Germany and Denmark.

"It sounds like you had your hands full. Leading fifty people must have been a real strain physically and mentally," says Clarence.

"Yes, it was. I don't think I will ever recover," responds Charles.

The skyline of New York comes into sight. Passing over The Bronx, Charles gets a view of his beloved Yankee Stadium. He knows he is finally home.

Charles pulls some paperwork out of his small carry bag. "Frida and Hans, here are your papers. These are the forgeries that Jean-Paul did for you two years ago. They are Danish passports with special entry visas from the U.S. State Department. I will be using my real U.S. passport. We should have no trouble getting through immigration with these." Or so he thinks.

The Marine Air Terminal is a small building at LaGuardia Field in Queens, NY. It is mostly used for domestic airboats and other small passenger planes.

Today an international military plane pulls up to one of its bays.

Charles, Hans, and Frida say their goodbyes and thank yous to Clarence.

They walk confidently up to the immigration desk and show their papers to the official standing there. He studies them carefully with a quizzical expression on his face. "Please wait here. I will be right back," he sternly says. He pulls aside a well-built attendant standing by his side, "Lou, watch them."

The official returns four minutes later with another official, obviously his superior. The senior official confronts Charles, "Are you Charles Levine?"

"Yes sir, is there a problem?" Charles asks.

"Are you attempting to bring these two people into the United States?"

"Yes, what is the issue?" Charles asks, now keenly aware that something has gone wrong.

"Mr. Levine, these papers are forgeries. You are under arrest. Lou, take them all away."

Alana Weinberg Levine sits in the airport's lounge, waiting to see her husband and brother. She will have to wait another night.

CHAPTER 3

August 1940

Charles and Hans spend the night in the men's facility at City Prison in lower Manhattan. Frida does the same at the women's facility. The next morning, Charles gets a visitor.

"What went wrong?" asks Bill Donovan. "I thought your forgeries were foolproof."

"I thought so too, but it looks like a missed little detail was our undoing. The cop taking me here told me the immigration official noticed a flaw in the visas. It seems we got the coloring of the back covers wrong—they were black, instead of navy blue."

"Damn, because of that minor error, you have caused a shit show at the Department of Justice. I did some questioning on my way here. They are charging you with attempting to smuggle illegal immigrants into the country. You are facing five years in jail for this offense."

"And Hans and Frida, what are their plans for them?"

"They will be deported back to their home country."

Charles is enraged. "You're got to be kidding. If they send them back to Germany, it is a death sentence. I am responsible for them being in this position. If anything happens to them, it will be on my conscience."

"Don't get overly agitated yet. I will do my best to get this situation resolved. I will see someone at the State Department tonight."

"It is outrageous that this is happening to me. I just saved the lives of fifty people. I should be considered a savior, not a criminal."

"The State Department is taking the violation of the quota laws very seriously. They are afraid if they make an exception for you, it will motivate others to try."

"You must see Roosevelt."

"I do not think that will work. Unfortunately, The President has not been sympathetic to Jewish refugees. Just last year he would not allow over nine hundred Jewish immigrants from the ocean liner, *St. Louis,* into the country. They were forced to return to Europe. Their fate is seriously in question."

"No, not Franklin. I know he is not always a friend to Jewish causes; I am talking about Eleanor. She is much more understanding. You must see her."

"Yes, I will do that."

"Bill, you are a true friend. I appreciate all that you are doing. But I need one additional favor. Please call my wife and tell her where I am. She must be worried sick."

"Will do."

CHAPTER 4

August 1940

Alana is led to the visiting area at City Prison. Five minutes later, Charles is escorted there, shackled in handcuffs and leg irons. It has been almost three years since they have seen each other.

Charles walks, as best he can, towards her. They embrace or, at least, she embraces him.

"Can you take these things off me?" Charles asks the guard. The guard, a surprisingly kind soul, removes the handcuffs.

Now unencumbered, Charles hugs and kisses Alana passionately. "My darling, I love you. I have missed you so much," he says.

Alana is bewildered. "Why are they doing this to you?"

"The government thinks I am a common criminal because I am trying to save two people. They have no compassion nor understanding for what we have been through. It's bad for me, but it can be even worse for Hans and Frida. They want to deport them back to Germany."

"They can't do that. The Nazis will kill them."

"I know that—but they don't seem to care."

"Where is Hans?"

"He is in the cell next to mine. I will try to get him." Charles walks over to the kind guard. "I need another favor. The prisoner, Hans Weinberg, can you bring him here? This is his sister. They have not seen each other in over fourteen years."

"That is highly unusual to have two inmates together, but I will see what I can do," the guard answers.

Charles and Alana wait patiently. Shortly Hans, also constrained, arrives. Alana runs to him. "I can't believe it. My little brother has grown into a big powerful man." They hug.

"Dear sister, it has been too long. I must tell you how grateful I am to you for sending your husband to Germany to save us. He is a brave man."

Charles, Alana, and Hans sit and bemoan their current situation for another half hour. The guard interrupts their conversation. "Your time is up. I must take the prisoners back to their cells now."

Upon parting, Charles speaks optimistically to Alana. "Don't worry darling, we will somehow get out of this mess, and I will be home in your arms once again."

Alana kisses Charles goodbye. "I hope you're right."

On the way back to their cells, Hans asks Charles, "Are you right? Are we going to get out of this?"

Charles answers honestly, "I have no idea how." Luckily for Charles, he has a friend in *Wild Bill*.

Bill Donovan spends the day in Washington D.C. speaking to attorneys at the Justice Department. He pleads his case for Charles for hours.

He then heads to the White House. He sees Eleanor—they talk for forty-five minutes. Summing up their conversation, Bill asks The First Lady one final question, "Do you think this plan will fly with him?"

Eleanor replies, "You know my husband is a stubborn son of a gun, but if he knows what is good for him, he will do what I want."

"That is all I can ask. Thank you," says Bill.

CHAPTER 5

August 1940

"I have spoken to the prosecutors, and I have a deal for you," says Bill to Charles at City Prison. It is the best you are going to get."

"Let's hear it," says Charles.

"You plead guilty, and you are sentenced to five years in prison."

"Stop right there. That's the best you can do? I go to prison for five years?"

"Let me finish. You are sentenced to five years. I did not say you will serve five years."

"OK, give me the full details."

"Hans and Frida are released immediately, and they can stay in the U.S. as legal immigrants, but Hans must join the military."

"That's ok. I don't think Hans will have any problem with that. If it comes to that, he will love to fight the Nazis."

"The next part of the deal is what I worked hard and long on. After serving only eight months you will get a Presidential Pardon."

Charles is surprised. He knows The President can be a hard ass. "Roosevelt has agreed to that?"

"No, not yet, but Eleanor is confident she will be able to convince Franklin it is the right thing to do."

"That is wonderful," says Charles. "Eleanor is a good person. She sees the big picture, whereas The President is often caught up in the politics of the time."

Charles contemplates going to jail again. "I don't relish jail time, but if Hans and Frida are free to live in this country, it will be worth it. Bill, you have done a great job. Thank you."

"Wait, there is more."

"I was afraid of that."

"The Justice Department is concerned about the precedent this case may set. So, we are telling the press a whole different story. We are telling them that you tried to smuggle Jewish business partners into the country through Mexico in an effort to profit by selling contraband in the form of tungsten powder. They will know about your arrest, conviction, and sentence. The pardon will be kept secret. You will have to live with your reputation being sullied."

"I can deal with that. My reputation since my last arrest was not so great anyhow. I, of course, agree to everything, but I do have one small stipulation."

"What could that be?"

"Before I am locked up, I would like to have at least one night to be alone with my wife. It has been three long years without any intimacy."

Bill happily agrees, "I am sure that will not be a problem. You deserve that."

CHAPTER 6

August 1940

The bailiff announces that the court is in session. "Federal Judge Donald Trainor is presiding."

"Everyone may be seated," says the judge. "The case in front of this court today is *The United States vs. Charles A. Levine.* Mr. Levine, please stand. You are charged with attempting to smuggle illegal immigrants and contraband into this country, class B felonies. How do you plead?"

"Guilty, your honor."

"Mr. Levine, these are very troubling times. These immigration laws were enacted to protect the citizens of our country. Your violation of this law is a serious offense. I am aware that the prosecutor and your attorneys have an understanding regarding your punishment. The terms are quite harsh. You are aware of this?" The judge is not privy to the proposed pardon.

"Yes, your honor. I am guilty and I am prepared to serve the time."

"Very well, I sentence you to five years confinement to be served at Sing Sing prison in Ossining, N.Y. The sentence is to begin in three days. You have two days to get your affairs in order and then report to the prison. Is that understood?"

Charles speaks up loud and clear, "Yes, your honor."

Charles and Alana walk out of the courtroom together. They are quite satisfied with the sentence, provided the pardon is forthcoming. "Alana, I am not happy I am going to be away from you for another eight months, but I can handle it with ease. Last time I was in jail, I was away for two years—that was difficult."

"Charles, I will be counting the days until you are free again to be with me. I will miss you dearly, but let's celebrate tonight. I have something special planned for you."

At their house in White Plains, Alana cooks a gourmet champagne dinner. Before they eat, though, Alana has something else in mind. She rips off the business attire worn at the courthouse exposing a sleek, revealing lingerie. "Darling, I've been waiting long enough for this moment," she says.

Charles is speechless at the sight of his beautiful wife in such a provocative outfit. He rushes to her, madly kissing her. As much as he likes the lingerie, he tears it off her. Alana does the same to his clothing. Right on the kitchen table, their bodies fuse together in furious sex. Nothing needs to be said.

After dinner, they continue to sip on the champagne, somewhat melancholily, knowing this will be their last dinner together for eight months. Alana serves Charles his favorite dessert, Boston Cream Pie.

"I can think of only one thing better than that dessert," says Charles with a twinkle in his eye and a smile on his face.

"And what might that be?" asks Alana, not so naively.

"You." They retire to the bedroom for an evening of intense lovemaking.

Hans and Frida are released from prison per their secret agreement the next day. They arrive bright and early at Alana's home.

"I'm glad you got here early. We have a lot to do," says Alana. "We are going to The Bronx for a full day of activities. I understand you want to go to the recruitment center to sign up with the army."

"If you don't mind, sis, we have another stop in mind first," says Hans.

Surprised, Alana asks, "Where would that be?"

Frida is quick to answer, "The Justice of the Peace. We want to get married."

"Oh, how wonderful," Alana exclaims. "Charles, come out of the bedroom, I have great news."

Charles walks into the kitchen. "Yes, what is it?"

"Let me tell him, says Frida. "I was not going to let my sister, Faye, beat me to the punch. I will be getting to the altar first. Hans and I are getting married today."

"Congratulations, I am so glad for you. You make a wonderful couple." Charles kisses Frida and shakes Hans' hand.

At the same courthouse where Charles and Alana tied the knot, Hans and Frida say their vows. All rejoice after the final "I do's."

The next stop is at the recruitment office. The marine sergeant at the front desk asks Hans, "What can I do for you today, young man?"

"I want to join the army," replies Hans.

"And why is that?" asks the sergeant.

"I want to kill Nazis."

"I can't blame you for wanting that, but you are a little premature. We are not at war yet."

"Sergeant, I come from Germany. What the Nazis have done there, and what they continue to do throughout Europe is inexcusable. I want to defend my faith against those horrors."

The sergeant is testing the mettle of the man in front of him. "That is admirable of you, but there is a lot of sentiment in this country to stay out of the war."

Hans' point of view cannot be shaken. "Lindbergh and his followers are blind. They do not comprehend the Nazis' evil ways. My faith is in the American people—they will soon see the need to fight and defend what is right."

"Son, you are exactly the type of man the army is looking for. We are not at war, but we are preparing for it. Which branch of the military are you thinking of?"

"I love airplanes. I would like to be a pilot in the Air Corps."

The sergeant takes out the enrollment papers. "Please sign here, and we'll see if we can do that for you."

Hans signs where necessary. He is so excited and trusting, he sees no need to read the paperwork.

The sergeant shakes Hans' hand. "Congratulations, welcome to the military. You have made the right decision. You report to Ft. Benning in Georgia in two days for your physical and to start training. The bus leaves from here at 10 a.m."

"I will be there. I am proud to be serving my new country."

Outside the office, Frida kisses her new husband. "You will make a great soldier," she says, unafraid of the dangers that might await him.

"Frida, you will stay with me while our husbands are away. I have plenty of room," says Alana.

Frida replies, "That is so nice. I will take you up on that, at least until I can find a place of my own."

"Now what?" asks Charles.

"We're going to have lunch," answers Alana.

"Where?"

Alana still works for The Yankees, and she is entitled to many perks. "I know of a place where they make the best hotdogs—Yankee Stadium. The Yankees play the Red Sox today, and I have box seats."

Charles' love of the game has not waned in the three years he has been out of the country. "I can think of no better place for my last night of freedom. I hear that Joe DiMaggio is a pretty good player."

After the game (the Yankees win 5-2 with Joe DiMaggio hitting two home runs), Alana drives all four of them to Sing Sing. Sadly, they say their goodbyes. Charles enters the gates of the prison.

CHAPTER 7

October 1940

The trip from Alana's house in White Plains to Sing Sing Prison is less than twenty miles. Alana makes the drive every Saturday to visit Charles.

"My dear, how are you doing?" Alana asks on her visit two months after Charles is imprisoned.

"As well as can be expected," he answers. "The conditions here are outrageously bad and there are some very mean criminals here. Murderers, rapists, and mob enforcers are just the worst of them. But I have made a few friends who are protecting me. I am safe."

"Thank God for that. I don't understand why they put you in such a maximum-level facility. You didn't do anything violent."

"I'm not quite sure why either, but it will be only for six more months. I can handle it. The less we moan about it, the better. Let's talk about what is going on in the outside world. I understand the War in Europe is not going well."

"No, it is not. Now that France has surrendered to Germany, Britain stands alone in the fight. London and other cities are being bombed regularly in what is being called The Blitz. There is a real fear that Britain will also fall."

"And we are still not helping?" Charles questions.

"Roosevelt is trying. He is now considered pro-war by his political opponents. He recently spearheaded a Destroyers for Bases deal, where the British Royal Navy gets fifty destroyers in exchange for land rights for U.S. military bases. He is also proposing a lend-lease agreement."

"I'm pleased he is finally doing something to help resist those damn Nazis."

"There are still many Americans who oppose our involvement and support an isolationist policy."

"And I bet Lindbergh is influencing that group with his pro-fascist views every chance he gets."

"Darling, you have enough to worry about in this awful place. Don't concern yourself with Lindbergh and The War. There is nothing you can do about it. I do have some good news to report. It looks like Hans is going to get his wish of becoming a pilot. He starts flight training next week."

"That is wonderful. I knew the army would appreciate his intelligence and ambition. He will be a great pilot."

At this point, a guard approaches them. "Let's wrap this visit up, you have only two more minutes," he says.

Charles asks one last question, "is there anything else we need to discuss?"

"It's funny you should ask. I decided to save the best for last. I'm pregnant! I'm due in May.

****

"I think I know who that baby is going to be," Alaine says cheerfully. "She is my mom!"

Charles gives no response. He only smiles and nods.

Alaine is curious. "What was my mother like as a baby?"

"I must assume your mom does not talk much about her childhood. The next sixteen months brought much heartache to our family. It is difficult for me to discuss, but I will do my best."

CHAPTER 8

March 1941

Charles languishes in Sing Sing for seven long months. He is anxious to know if his pardon is forthcoming, as promised. Hopefully, Bill Donovan will have good news when he visits.

Wild Bill arrives at the appointed hour. "Hi Charles, how are you doing?" he asks.

"How do you think I'm doing? I'm miserable. My wife is seven months pregnant; I should be with her. Is the paperwork for my pardon in the works?"

"I am confident everything will go as planned, eventually. Roosevelt is very busy, as you can imagine."

"I don't want to hear—eventually. I want to hear—now."

"I will speak to Eleanor today. I promise you."

"We do not have much leeway with this. I must be out of here in time to witness the birth of my child."

"I fully understand."

245

Bill places a phone call to the White House. "Eleanor, do you remember Charles Levine is due to get his pardon next month?"

"I have not forgotten. Charles Levine is a hero in my book. He should not have been imprisoned in the first place. I have already spoken with the Justice Department. The paperwork should be ready any day. I will put it under Franklin's nose and force him to sign it. It will get done. But remember the pardon must be kept secret."

"I understand. Thank you for all your help."

Three days later, the warden of Sing Sing receives a "Top Secret" package from the White House. Inside it is a Presidential Pardon effective at the end of the month.

On March 31, Charles Levine walks out of the prison—a free man. He is greeted with hugs and kisses by his wife.

PART VIII: THE CAREGIVER

CHAPTER 1

May 1941

Charles and Alana have never been happier as they await the birth of their child. They have been apart for so long and now they hope to live blissfully a long time as a family.

At 6:30 p.m. on May 11, Alana gives birth to a healthy baby girl named Edith. It should be the happiest day of their lives. It is not.

After the birth of Edith, Dr. Parsons, the physician who delivers the baby, pulls Charles aside. "I have some very bad news."

"There is something wrong with the baby?" Charles questions.

"No, as far as we can tell at this early stage, the baby appears to be fine. The problem is with your wife."

Charles sits down to hear the bad news. "What is it?"

"During the delivery, my nurses and I discovered some serious issues. It most likely should have been detected earlier, during the pregnancy, but it was not."

Dr. Parsons pauses. The doctor has been practicing for many years, but it is never easy to relay a bad prognosis. "Alana has advanced breast cancer. It has metastasized throughout her body. There is nothing we can do---her condition is fatal. We estimate she will only have another six months to live. I am so sorry."

Charles is shaken by the news. He almost falls off his chair. He mutters out a question, "Have you told my wife?"

"No, I will leave that up to you."

CHAPTER 2

June---December 1941

Charles cares for the baby and Alana. He does a magnificent job of providing for their every need, with the assistance of Frida, who is still living in their home. For the baby, he does the feedings, the changing of the diapers, and the comforting during the bouts of crying.

Alana's condition worsens as the days pass. Her pain becomes unbearable. Charles holds her tightly, sometimes for hours on end. He is always by her bedside.

Near the end, she can hardly talk at all. She struggles to get out a few words. In a whisper, she says, "Charles, promise me that Edith will have a good home. If you cannot manage, I will understand."

Charles takes her hand in his and gently strokes her head. "My dearest Alana, I love you and I love Edith. I promise you I will always do what is best for our child."

December 7, 1941: "*A date which will live in infamy.*" It is so for the country, and it is so for the Levine/Weinberg families.

249

Alana Levine passes away at her home in the early afternoon with her husband at her side. "Charles, I am so sorry. Alana was a wonderful person," says Frida.

Fighting to talk through his tears, Charles responds, "Thank you. She was a great wife and would have been a great mother. It is a pity she did not live long enough to have the pleasure of raising Edith."

"Let us mourn together," says Frida. They both lower their heads in prayer.

Frida cannot mourn for Alana for long. Not an hour after Alana dies, news reaches the East Coast about the Japanese attack on Pearl Harbor in Hawaii. Hans Weinberg is stationed there.

Frida must now turn her concern to the well-being of her husband. "The news on the radio about the Pearl Harbor attack by the Japanese is ominous. I am worried sick about Hans. I hope he is alright," she says to Charles.

Hans is not alright. Shortly before 8 a.m. (Hawaiian time) The Pearl Harbor base is attacked by Japanese planes shelling torpedoes, bombs, and bullets at U.S. Navy battleships. Hans and the other pilots are asleep in their barracks. At the first sounds of the attack, they rush to their planes hoping to defend their base with return fire.

Hans never makes it to his plane. He is sprayed with bullets, shot from the sky, and falls to the ground ten yards from his aircraft.

Hans is alive but seriously injured. His left leg is riddled with bullets, and he has internal injuries to his lung and spleen. The doctors decide that his leg must be amputated, and his spleen removed for him to survive. He will never get his chance to fight the Germans or the Japanese.

Frida receives the news of her husband's condition by telegram. "Oh my god, my poor husband. I must get to him right away."

Charles, though grieving for his loss, is understanding. "Yes, you must."

"I am catching the next train to San Francisco. From there the military is providing me with a flight to Honolulu. I am so sorry I cannot be here for you in your hours of grief."

"Do not fret, I will manage."

CHAPTER 3

December 1941

Charles makes the short drive to the Westchester Hills Cemetery to say his final goodbyes to Alana. With him is Babe Ruth, who is retired from baseball, but is still Charles' good friend. Edith has been left at home, cared for by a friendly neighbor.

"I am so sorry for your loss. Everyone in the Yankee's office appreciated her charm and humor," says *The Babe.*

"Thank you, Babe. She will be missed."

The rabbi gives a stirring eulogy, followed by a few short words from Charles. Tears flow from both men.

Other than the rabbi, Charles and Babe are the only two attendees at the funeral until a striking, well-dressed, young woman appears near the end of the service and approaches Charles.

"Hello, Dad. My deepest condolences for your loss," the woman says as she lovingly puts her arms around Charles.

Charles is shocked. It has been eight years since he last saw his eldest daughter from his first marriage. "Eloise, my dear, what a wonderful surprise. I have missed you so much. Thank you for coming today."

"I recently turned twenty-one and all restrictions about seeing you are now lifted. I wish it was under better circumstances, but I saw the obituary in *The New York Times*. I have missed you so much, and I thought this might be the right time for a reunion."

"You thought right. Many times, I thought to seek you out, but I was afraid of your mother's wrath. I have always loved my children, and I am so pleased that on this very sad day, you have come to put a little happiness into my life."

The Babe interrupts their conversation, "It is nice to see the two of you back together. I have a personal appearance to do in Manhattan---I will grab a taxi. You guys now will have time alone to catch up. Goodbye."

Eloise and Charles decide to have lunch at a nearby diner. "I have read about your troubles in the papers," says Eloise. "I thought you were given a long prison sentence?"

"It's a long story. Let's just say, I was able to get a quick release. But tell me about yourself. You look like you have done very well."

"I have been fortunate. I married a successful attorney three years ago. We live in a fabulous apartment in the city."

"And your mom and sister—how are they?"

"Mom remarried about five years ago. Ardith is a senior in high school. They live a comfortable life in Great Neck, L.I."

"That is wonderful. I have no bitter feelings towards Grace. I am so glad everything seems to have worked out for the best. I do have a piece of news you might be surprised about—you have a new half-sister. My late wife gave birth seven months ago to a beautiful baby girl, named Edith."

"Wow, that is a surprise—I'm so happy for you. My husband, Rick, and I have been trying to have children since we first got married. The doctors have told me it is unlikely I will ever give birth." Eloise's expression turns sullen.

"That is a shame, but don't give up hope." A thought pops into Charles's head, but he decides to keep it to himself. "I would like to meet your husband. Let's make a dinner date."

"That is a great idea. I have told Rick all about your exploits. He would love to learn more about your aviation stories. I will make a reservation in a restaurant near us. How is Thursday night?"

"That will be perfect. I look forward to it."

CHAPTER 4

December 1941

Charles meets Eloise and Rick Rosenthal at the famous 21 Club on 52nd Street on December 11. Rick is dressed in an expensive suit, with a silk tie and gold cufflinks. It is obvious that Rick is a man of means. Eloise has indeed been fortunate.

Rick starts the conversation with the news of the day. "Congress declared war on Germany today. It takes an attack by the Japanese to convince us Americans that is the right course of action. Those Nazis are killing Jews and for too long we do nothing. I understand you have had some scuffles with Germans yourself."

"I don't want to get too deep into that, but yes, I did encounter some difficult times in Germany and Denmark. Let's hope our entry into this horrible war can soon put an end to the atrocities that Europe and Asia have endured," replies Charles.

"I'll drink to that," says Eloise. They all raise a glass of wine.

After dessert, Charles decides the time is right to discuss a difficult subject. "I am saddened to learn from Eloise that you are having difficulty in starting a family. If you don't mind me asking, what is the problem?"

Rick answers quickly, "No, we don't mind discussing it. After all, you are family. Eloise has endometriosis—which is a condition that prevents a woman from carrying a fetus to full term. It is very doubtful that it can be cured. We have resigned ourselves to looking into adoption."

"I might have a solution. As you are aware, I recently became a father again, but without a wife, it will be very difficult for me to care for little Edith properly. Would you be interested in becoming foster parents for her?"

Eloise and Rick look at each other. Big smiles come across both their faces. They don't have to discuss the question. "Yes," they both say simultaneously.

"I don't want to give up Edith entirely. I love her and giving her to you is the hardest thing I will ever do. I plan to visit occasionally. But I do not have the means nor the ability to see to her needs. The dying wish of my wife was that Edith would be taken care of in a good home. I am confident that you two can do this."

Eloise jumps up from her seat and hugs her dad. "Thank you so much, you have made us so happy. You can be assured we will raise Edith well."

****

"My mother never told me she was raised by her half-sister. Why is that?" asks Alaine.

"I'm not quite sure, but I have my suspicions. You do know you were named after your natural grandmother, Alana?" asks Charles.

"No, I didn't know that either. Why have all these secrets been kept from me?"

"Your father is no fan of mine, and he feels I have told you much that is untrue. He is wrong, but I think my stories should now end."

"No, you can't stop now. You have been with so many famous people. You must tell me what became of them all."

"It is true, many of my friends and associates were people of renown, and they are all gone now. For reasons only God possesses I have outlived them all."

"The saddest story is of Amelia Earhart. As I told you before, she goes missing on a flight around the globe in July of 1937.   There are many theories of what happened. The most prevailing one is she runs out of gas, crashes, and dies somewhere in the Pacific Ocean. She was declared dead in January 1939. It was such a tragedy to lose someone so young and full of life."

"*The Babe* died in 1948 of throat cancer. He was a great friend and a once-in-a-lifetime ballplayer."

"Mable Boll marries for the fifth time. This time not for money but for love, to an unemployed harp player. She attempts a comeback in a one-woman show on Broadway in 1940. It is an abysmal failure. She died all alone in a psychiatric hospital in 1949. It was a sad ending for a woman once so captivating."

"Joe Bellanca, my ex-partner, continues to design planes. He appears on the cover of *Time Magazine* because of his innovative concepts. During WW II his planes are favored by pilots for their stability and range. He died in 1960 of Leukemia. Posthumously he was inducted into the Aviation Hall of Fame. He was a talented man."

"Clarence Chamberlin, my pilot on our flight to Berlin, will always be known for his many historic flights.

After training pilots for action in WW2, he retires. He died in 1976."

"Do you remember Lloyd Bertaud? He was the pilot that I fired, and he then put an injunction on *The Columbia* that prevented me from being the first to fly transatlantic to Paris. Well, he never receives a dollar for his troubles. Shortly after my trip to Berlin, he takes off over the Atlantic Ocean, crashes, and is killed. No big loss there."

"Bruno Hauptmann is tried, convicted, and executed in 1936 for the murder of Charles Lindbergh Jr. Good riddance—he got what he deserved.

"Wild Bill Donovan becomes a trusted ally of President Roosevelt. During the war, he heads the Office of Strategic Services (OSS), the first U.S. intelligence agency. He is considered the father of the CIA. He died in 1959 of illnesses related to dementia."

"Pierre/Jean-Paul (I never did learn his real name), my forger, is captured by the Germans but escapes from a prison camp near the end of the war. He died in 1986 at the age of 101 from natural causes."

"Neils Bohr escapes the Nazis in 1943 and comes to the United States. There he helps in the design of the atomic bombs that end The War.   He died, in Denmark, in 1962 from heart failure."

"The smartest person I ever met was Eleanor Roosevelt. After the death of her husband, she remains an important force. She continues to fight for civil rights and against antisemitism. In 1946 she becomes the first chairperson of the United Nations Commission on Human Rights. She passed away in 1962 due to cardiac arrest."

"Grandpa, you failed to discuss someone—Charles Lindbergh."

"Just the mention of his name makes me sick. While I was on a quest to save lives, he continues his agenda of appeasement, isolation, and hate. After the attack on Pearl Harbor, the America First Committee is disbanded. He softens his admiration of Nazism, but never recants his anti-Semitic viewpoints. After his death in 1974, a lot more information is uncovered to prove what a low-life and fiend he was."

"How so?" asks Alaine.

"Remember I told you that Bruno Hauptmann had an accomplice in the murder of the baby, Charles Lindbergh Jr. There is a lot of speculation that the accomplice was none other than Charles Lindbergh himself."

"How could that be? Why would a father kill his child?"

"Lindbergh, as I have said many times, was a strange individual. A multitude of his views were idiotic. Before I get into his motives, let me list the circumstances that have led many people to believe he had a role in the murder:

1) He had a speaking engagement the evening of the kidnapping which he cancelled, something he never did.

2) It was a Tuesday night. Only the family and the servants knew they would be in that home in New Jersey that night. They usually only stayed there on the weekends.

3) Lindbergh ordered the entire household to stay out of the nursery between the hours of 8 p.m. and 10 p.m. (the hours of the kidnapping). He had never given those instructions before.

4) The ladder used to get to the window of the nursery was four feet short. Someone would have had to hand the child to Hauptmann.

5) Oddly, the police allowed Lindbergh to supervise the investigation. He purposely hid from the authorities all clues that might point to an inside job.

6) He refused to allow the FBI to assist in the investigation.

7) The motive is the most damning piece of evidence against Lindbergh. The baby suffered from Rickets,

a disease that often leads to deformities such as an oddly shaped skull as a child grows older. If you recall, Lindbergh was a strong advocate of eugenics. He believed that the world would be a better place if only the strongest and best survived and the weakest and inferior were eliminated. In his warped mind, no child of his should exist if it is not perfect in every way."

"That is sick!" exclaims Alaine.

"I know it sounds crazy, but that is what he believed in, but there is more. Lindbergh was supposedly an upstanding family man, always loyal to his wife, Anne. It is not true.

Starting in 1957, Lindbergh travels often to Europe without his wife. There, he is a busy man. He has extensive sexual relationships with not one, not two, but three mistresses. These affairs result in him becoming the father of seven illegitimate children. He attempts to keep these nefarious, illicit unions a secret, but eventually, the truth comes out. In addition to all his other faults, he is a philanderer and a cad.

And that, my child, brings to an end the story of my life and my associations."

"Grandpa, your stories cannot end---there must be more."

"The history books tell the rest of this sad story. Germany and Japan were defeated by the Allied forces, but not before six million Jews were exterminated. The Holocaust was a tragedy the whole world should be ashamed of. Every country including the U.S. was at fault. They stood idly by while the Germans did this most horrific genocide. Asylum was needed but none was granted. I only regret that I did not do more."

"You did all you could," says Alaine proudly. "But after the war, there are still fifty more years of your life. What happens to you doing those years.?"

"Sadly, not much. The death of Alana causes me to fall into a deep depression that I never recover from. I work for the CIA and Bill Donovan as a confidential informant from time to time. I am involved in Cuba at the time of the fall of Bautista and the rise of Castro, and with the debacle at the Bay of Pigs. That is another long story. But mostly I drift from job to job in obscurity.

For the last twenty years, I lived on and off the streets, in friends' homes, and in homeless shelters. Perhaps that is why your mother told you little about me and her upbringing. She was ashamed."

"I am not ashamed—I am proud to be your granddaughter. I love you." Alaine hugs Charles deeply.

"I enjoyed our talks. You have made the last days of an old, sick man enjoyable, but I have lived long enough. Thank you for being my friend."

Charles closes his eyes, takes one last breath, and passes away, at peace.

Who is Charles Levine?

PART IX: THE DECEASED

CHAPTER 1

December 1991

Alaine is inconsolable. Her grandfather dies by her side. For this eleven-year-old, as it would be for anyone her age, it is a horrifying, emotional event. She had grown very close to him.   Her tears fall throughout the night. In the morning her mother tries her best to calm her.

"My sweetheart, your grandfather, my father, lived a very long life—it was his time. You filled the last few days of his life with joy by listening to his stories. You should be commended for making those days for him as comfortable as possible. I know he appreciated it. We now all must mourn his loss," says Edith.

Alaine attempts to wipe away her tears. "Mom, you have never discussed your relationship with him in any detail. Nor have you told me about being raised by your half-sister. What's the story?"

"It is complicated. When I was old enough to understand, I, at first, was bitter that I did not have a natural father and mother in my life. As I matured, I grew to know the reasons, and I became comfortable with my situation. My foster parents, Eloise and Rick, were wonderful to me. They treated me as a natural daughter, and I accepted them as my natural parents. I even called them *Mom and Dad* and I took their last name as my own.

As the years passed, Charles recognized that his presence only complicated our family dynamic. He visited less often, and, as a result, my relationship with him suffered. By the time I was a teenager, he was out of my life. It broke his heart, but for my sake, he let it happen."

Edith pauses to collect her thoughts. "I know now he loved me, and I am only sorry I did not reach out sooner to help him. When I found out he was living in a homeless shelter, I had to take him in to live with us."

"And why am I first being told about all this now?"

"Your father thought it best to wait until you were a little older to hear everything. I was remiss in not disagreeing with him more firmly. I did get my way, however, in naming you after your natural grandmother."

Alaine sits silently absorbing her mom's explanations and excuses.

Philip Pollack, Alaine's father, obvious to all, does not have close feelings regarding the life and death of Charles Levine. As Alaine attempts to stop her crying, he comes to her room.

"Alaine, I know this is a difficult day for you, but we must move on." In an alarming lack of understanding for her grief, he continues. "Your grandfather was not the man he told you he was. He is not deserving of a full day of your tears."

Alaine is distraught. Angrily, she responds, "Why do you say that? What proof do you have that he was lying to me? I believed every word and nothing you can say will change my mind."

"Alaine, I wish it was all true. Throughout your life, I want you to believe that people are good and trustworthy. But you will learn that is not always the case. Your grandfather is a prime example. First, he deserted his family, not once, but twice."

"That is not true. With his first wife, they split mutually because of his financial setbacks. She was the one who insisted he have no contact with his children. And Mom told me about her childhood. He made sure she had a good home because he could not provide for her. He fulfilled the dying wish of his wife, and, out of love, much to his regret, removed himself from her life."

"Darling, you are seeing these tales through the eyes of a child. An adult, like me, sees it another way."

"Your way is wrong!"

"That is questionable, but I will move on. His association with all these famous people simply is not true. There is not a person alive that can verify any of it. In addition, his supposed fame surrounding his aviation career was grossly exaggerated. And his obsession with the viewpoints of Charles Lindbergh, to my mind, was over the top."

"Dad, I have heard enough from you. I get it—you did not like him."

"I want you to know the truth. There are more things I need to say. His story about saving Jews from the Nazis is pure fabrication. I have done some research and have found newspaper articles about Charles. He was arrested and jailed for five years for smuggling contraband and illegal immigrant accomplices into the country. Those are the facts."

"Your facts are wrong. I stand behind what Grandpa told me. I have no way to prove it, but my belief in him is strong."

"Sweetheart, I admire your loyalty to him, but it is misplaced. I hate to talk poorly of the dead, but he was a scoundrel, a grifter, and a liar. I am convinced."

Alaine's tears return.

Edith's foster parents, Eloise and Rick Rosenthal, are alive and well, living in Palm Beach, Florida. Edith places a call to them.

"Hi Mom, I have some bad news. Our father has passed away," says Edith.

"Oh, how sad. He lived a long life. I would like to say a good one, but it was certainly eventful. We all know he had his ups and downs. I will miss his stories. Is there going to be a funeral?" asks Eloise.

"Yes, a small one. There are not many left who knew him. It is in two days---on the ninth."

"We will be there, and I will make a few calls. There are some others I am sure would like to pay their respects."

"That's nice of you. I will see you then."

CHAPTER 2

December 1991

At the Goldsmith Funeral Parlor, the funeral of Charles A. Levine starts promptly at 11 a.m. In attendance are Alaine Pollack, Philip and Edith Pollack, and Eloise and Rick Rosenthal.

As the rabbi makes his opening remarks two other couples enter the room and take their seats. The four new attendees are two men, appearing to be in their seventies, one of whom has a prosthetic leg and walks with the aid of a cane, and two attractive women, also in their seventies, who look remarkably alike. The Pollack family look at each other—they have no idea who the new arrivals are.

After the rabbi says his perfunctory words, Alaine is called to the podium to give a eulogy. She is poised and confident. Her speech is brief but impassioned.

"My grandfather, Charles Levine, meant many things to many people. To me, he was a dear friend. I only got to know him during the last week of his life, but in that short time, we became very close. He told me the tales of his life which are stories of adventure, heroism, love, and friendship. I believe them all. Others, (she looks directly at her father,) are not as sure of their accuracy."

Alaine stops momentarily for effect. "He was a man who took chances in many different endeavors. Some were successful, others were not, but he always tried his best. His fights against antisemitism and the people who spread it are especially noteworthy. History will judge his accomplishments and his failures, but, in this girl's mind, he will come out way ahead. I love you Grandpa and I will miss you dearly."

Alaine walks proudly from the stage. Her mother greets her. They embrace.

The mourners walk out of the room after the ceremony. The one-legged man stops to introduce himself to Alaine. "Hello Alaine, my name is Hans Weinberg. I am your great uncle---your grandmother, Alana Levine, was my sister. Your eulogy was wonderful, and you are correct—his stories are true. Don't let anyone tell you otherwise—I have the proof you need."

CHAPTER 3

December 1991

After the burial at the nearby cemetery, everyone retreats to the Pollack home for the shiva.

Eloise explains all the connections. "Through the years, I tried my best to keep in touch with all of my father's relatives. Hans and his wife, Frida, live in Hawaii and Frida's twin sister, Faye, and her husband, Jonas, live in Denmark. I notified all of them of Charles' passing. They all felt, despite their long flights, they had to be at the funeral."

Edith says, "We have heard your names, but we would love to know more about you and your time with Charles."

Hans speaks for the group. "After the attack on Pearl Harbor, I spent many months recovering from my injuries. My wife, Frida, came to my bedside and didn't leave. After the war ended, we loved Hawaii so much that we decided to make it our home. We proudly became U.S. citizens, raised two children, and became grandparents of five. And yes, I have many stories to share about Charles."

Frida adds, "My sister and brother-in-law, Faye and Jonas, likewise have a large family. They have three children and eight grandchildren. Later they will tell you their story, but first let's eat—I'm starving."

After their meal, everyone sits down in the living room, curious to hear more from their newfound friends.

"Philip, I understand you have your doubts about Charles' wartime exploits," says Hans. "Well, we are living proof that he was telling the truth. Without his brave efforts to get us out of Germany, none of us would be alive today. We give thanks every day, as do my children, and when they are old enough, so will my grandchildren. In addition, fifty Jewish families are living in Sweden and around the world with an untold number of children and grandchildren who also have Charles to thank for saving their lives. He is and always will be our hero."

Faye now speaks up. "Jonas and I stayed in Denmark, and just as Charles predicted, in late 1943, the Nazis came hunting for all the Jews remaining there. Through the efforts of the resistance, including my husband, and his father, approximately 95% of the eight thousand Jews living in Denmark were able to escape to Sweden. It was a miracle that so many were able to survive."

Jonas now speaks up, "They used the same method of utilizing small fishing boats to cross *The Sound* (albeit on a much larger scale) that Charles had devised. Unfortunately, my father, Dr. Karl Baum was not among the survivors. He stayed in Denmark to continue to treat his patients. Ultimately, he was captured by the Nazis and killed in a concentration camp."

Alaine ecstatically exclaims, "You see Dad, I was right—Charles was a hero!"

Philip humbly responds. "I stand corrected. I am man enough to admit I was wrong. It does appear that Charles did these brave, heroic acts, much to my surprise. But I stand behind my belief that many of his associations were not true."

Edith angrily lashes out at her husband. "Philip, give it up. This is a day of mourning. Give some credit to the deceased. Your daughter is smart enough to appreciate this man's life. Why are you so stubborn?"

"Until some proof is shown to me, I will not relent," says Philip.

"Be careful what you wish for," says Hans as he pulls out a large suitcase. "Through the years Charles sent me many mementos which he asked me to keep safe. In this bag are those items. Alaine, Charles recently sent me a letter leaving all the contents of this bag to you, so will you do us the honor of showing everyone what is inside."

"It will be my pleasure." Alaine picks up the bag and peers in. "First, there is a baseball. The inscription reads: *To my good friend and greatest fan, Charles Levine.* It is signed *The Babe.* Attached to it is a letter of authenticity." Alaine holds the baseball up for everyone to see.

"Next is a program. It says: *M.I.T. is proud to present AMELIA EARHART speaking on THE FUTURE OF AVIATION.* It is signed: *To my new friend, Charles Levine, good luck with your aviation career, AMEILIA.*

"Can I see it?" asks Philip. Alaine hands the program to her father. "Yes, I must admit, it looks genuine."

"There is a lot more in here," says Alaine. She picks up a publication for everyone to see. "It reads: *PLAYBILL—MABLE BOLL Staring in QUEEN OF DIAMONDS.* It is signed: *To my King Charles from your Queen, I love you, MABLE.*"

"Impressive," says Edith.

"Next is a *PROCLAMATION* on heavy parchment paper. It reads: *The Nation of Germany hereby grants to CHARLES LEVINE the award of GALANT MERIT in*

277

honor of his heroic flight on June 5, 1927, to Berlin. Signed, PRESIDENT PAUL VON HINDENBURG."

"Frida and I were there the day he landed," says Faye. "We were only kids. His achievement was special---everyone was awestruck."

Alaine continues, "Wait the best is yet to come. There is a gold plaque inscribed with the words: *On behalf of the DENMARK RESISTANCE FIGHTERS, we salute CHARLES LEVINE for his courage and inspiration in support of the JEWISH community. Thank you, Dr. Karl Baum and Neils Bohr."*

"My father and Neils Bohr considered Charles to be a great friend and ally," says Jonas.

"Next, I have an old telegram dated April 22, 1941. Alaine holds the paper high. "It reads: *To The Aviator, CONGRATULATIONS, you are a free man. I knew Eleanor and Franklin would come through for you. Your efforts to overcome all the obstacles and persevere to thwart the Nazis at every turn were remarkable. It was my pleasure to work with you and I look forward to your help in future escapades. Your friend, THE WILD ONE, BILL DONOVAN."*

Alaine takes a letter out of an envelope. "Finally, there is a letter on expensive-looking stationery."

"May I read this one?" asks Hans.

"Of course," answers Alaine.

"I spoke to Charles when he sent me this last item," says Hans. "He was very proud to receive it and he considered it the most important memento in his collection. The heading simply reads: **THE WHITE HOUSE,** it is dated **March 10, 1941**.

> *Dear Charles,*
>
> *I am compelled to write this letter in appreciation of your brave efforts. You have saved over fifty Jews from certain death at the hands of the horrible Nazi regime. You are deserving of a medal--- instead of imprisonment.*
>
> *If I had my way the U.S. would have granted asylum to all Jewish refugees with open arms. But it was not to be. Unfortunately, because of political and economic considerations, my husband refused to back down on this matter. I apologize for him and the nation for this outrageous mistake.*
>
> *As you know, we have planted a phony story in the newspapers about an illegal smuggling. I regret you have served some prison time to silence any claims of favoritism, but your Presidential Pardon will be forthcoming. For reasons, I am sure you can*

appreciate, this letter and the Pardon must be kept secret until after Franklin and I have passed away.

Best of luck, always.

Eleanor Roosevelt

First Lady of the United States.

Everyone remains speechless for a few seconds, overwhelmed by the written words of the most acclaimed First Lady.

Alaine breaks the silence, "Dad, is this the proof you were asking for?"

Philip slowly walks over to his daughter and puts his arms around her. "I am so sorry. I was a fool, and you were right all along. Charles was an honorable man. He is deserving of all our praise, and should be fondly remembered for his deeds, friendships, and bravery."

Who is Charles Levine?

Acknowledgments

With grateful thanks, I acknowledge Bonnie and Robert Tarlowe for turning me on to their long-forgotten relative, Charles Levine. Their introduction started me on this exciting path.

The following people provided input, support, and assistance: Lee Weitzman, Larry Parsont, Robert Klamkin, Joel Gazes, and Linda & Mark Lipshutz. A well-deserved thank you goes out to them all.

Finally, my dear wife, Adrienne, is always there to add a kind word of support. Her help and patience are inspirational—it is much appreciated.

About the Author

Jeffrey Saporta, a retired lawyer and real estate manager, was born in New York City in 1949. He now lives in Florida with his wife of fifty years, Adrienne. They have two children, Jonathan and Meredith. Jeff is an avid golfer and a loyal fan of the NY Mets & NY Jets. This is his third novel. For more information about this book or the author email: jls1149@gmail.com

Who is Charles Levine?

Who is Charles Levine?

Who is Charles Levine?

Printed in Great Britain
by Amazon

34614256R00163